An excerpt from Cait and the Devil

"What were you doing in here?" The quiet, controlled tone of his voice belied the anger bubbling beneath.

"I—I fell asleep. I'm sorry. I didn't mean to."

"You have your own room. Your own bed to sleep in," he reminded her tightly. "I'll ask you once again. What were you doing in here?"

"I just... I came in to look...to see if you were here. I hadn't seen you all day."

"There is a reason for that. I'm a very busy man and I don't have time to act as playmate to my wife. If you wish for company you can look for it elsewhere. I'm sure the women of the keep will be happy to comply."

"Oh," she murmured miserably.

"My men have been combing the woods for you for an hour. They have been over every inch of the castle and grounds in search of you—"

"I was right here!"

"Don't interrupt me," he snapped, "or things will go very badly for you. I assigned a guard to you so I would know at all times that you are safe. He is now in grave dishonor because of your capricious behavior. I don't care what you decide to do, but from now on, if you leave your room your guard is to know exactly where you are. Do you understand me?"

"But, sir—"

"Do you understand?" he barked.

She bowed her head. "Yes."

Cait

and the

Devil

A historical BDSM fantasy by

Annabel Joseph

Other erotic romance by Annabel Joseph

Mercy
Firebird
Deep in the Woods
Fortune
Owning Wednesday
Lily Mine
Comfort Object
Caressa's Knees
Odalisque
Cirque du Minuit
Burn For You

Erotica by Annabel Joseph

Club Mephisto
Molly's Lips: Club Mephisto Retold

Coming soon:

Command Performance
The Edge of the Earth (as Molly Joseph)
Disciplining the Duchess

About this book

As a long time reader of historical romance novels, I yearned to create a story that contained all my most favorite romance elements: the tortured, gruff hero, the painfully innocent but plucky heroine, the evil villain, long lost relatives and meddling servants, secrets and hidden alliances and a liberal sprinkling of magic and mystery. I also wanted to introduce power exchange into the mix—no small feat in a medieval Scotland setting, but something I wanted to attempt nonetheless. Cait and the Devil was the result of this singular experiment.

Admittedly, this novel is more of whimsy and fantasy than historical accuracy, but I hope you will enjoy Cait and Duncan's story just the same.

For Jeff
I'll love you forever

Chapter One

Cait shifted on her horse. The endless journey was growing more and more difficult to take. If she only knew they were near, she could bear it better, but none of the soldiers talked to her or so much as looked her way. It felt like she was traveling to the end of the world; that wherever they were going got farther and farther away. She'd lost count of the days now, although she guessed it was nearly two weeks she'd been on the back of a blasted horse.

Patience, Cait, she could hear Erma saying quietly in her ear. It was as if her nurse was still there beside her even though it had been nearly a month since she passed. *If only. If only.* If only Erma hadn't died, she might yet be living happily in their cozy cottage in the wilds of Aberdeen, instead of traveling to Inverness to be wed to a man she'd never met.

Her hair stood up on the back of her neck as it always did when she remembered. She was traveling to be *married,* married to a stranger with the unfortunate name of the Devil of Inverness. Cait had no desire to marry at all, much less be married to a devil, and for that reason she remembered as infrequently as possible that she was traveling to be made a bride. But forgetting didn't make anything different. Forgetting didn't make any of it go away.

She wished she could forget Erma dying. Forget that lonely journey to find help, only to learn at Aberdeen's castle that she was the k
ing's own daughter. The king's *bastard*, unwanted and despised. His eyes had narrowed when she'd been hauled before him. He hadn't looked on her with anything akin to fatherly love.

"I thought you died," was all he'd said. "I was told you died. Your mother tells lies."

"I don't have a mother, sir."

"You certainly do," he'd snapped, "and that noxious slut glories in making my life miserable even to this day. Even to this hour," he said, looking down his long nose at her, his lips twitching in disgust. "I've no doubt you're as much a meddlesome slut as she. What is your name? What is your age?"

"Caitlyn, sir. And I turned seventeen at the end of January."

"Of course you did. Well, seventeen is old enough to be married, is it not? That will get you out of my hair," he added under his breath, turning to look at a nearby advisor.

"The earl of Inverness, the younger. Douglas's son. His name escapes me, but they call him the Devil. You know of whom I speak?"

"Lord Niall?"

"No, the other. The bastard son with the white hair."

"Lord Duncan?"

"That's the one. Did he not recently lose a wife in childbirth?"

"Yes, sire."

"Very well. Send this girl to Inverness to take her place. Tell the Devil earl I order him to wed her. A bastard for a bastard." He laughed coldly. "They will understand each other, will they not?"

"Yes, sire," said the advisor, his eyes flicking briefly to Cait and then away. "I'll arrange for transport of your daughter at once."

"Yes, at once," the King demanded. "I want her gone as soon as possible. Her strange looks disquiet me. And do not bother with a big retinue. She is not valuable to me. If I get my wish, Duncan will dispatch this one in childbirth too, then this thing will be done which should have been done long ago."

Cait listened to all this kneeling before him, listened to the soul-numbing words from the mouth of the man who had fathered her. She'd never known he existed until this awful day. Of course she had imagined sometimes what sort of man her father was. If he was a kind man. If he ever wondered where she was. Now she knew the truth about him and wished she didn't. It hurt her to hear him call her mother a slut, and to wish Cait gone so she needn't pain him with her awful looks. The entire conversation had hurt, but nothing quite so much as his cold, plain hatred for her existence.

Cait was not a vain girl. She knew she was no beauty. She knew her looks were unappealing and strange. Her hair was so black, her eyes so light; her skin so pale and translucent. She had not a trace of her father's golden blond hair and deep brown eyes. But must he hate her so without even knowing her? She tried to be pleasant and agreeable to everyone she met. She had cared for her old nurse Erma like her own mother. She could garden and keep house. She tried to keep busy and live happily and hurt no one or nothing on earth. She had never been hurt either, not as her father had hurt her that day. She'd never been cut so carelessly and so deep, and to have it come at the hands of her own father was terrible. She cried for hours afterward though no one took notice. Before nightfall she'd been lifted summarily onto the back of a horse.

And now here she was, journeying endlessly to Inverness. She doubted the men with her cared whether she lived or died. For a long while she'd feared they would ride out with her some distance and kill her and leave her body for the wolves, at her father's command. It soon became obvious, though, that they would never journey this far just to slay someone and leave them to rot. Perhaps they were riding with her into the wilderness to abandon her, to let her wander lost and starving until she died. As it was, they barely took a care for her needs, or fed her. If one of them spoke to her, it was little more than a grunt. If she reached her future husband's keep alive it would be a miracle. Some days she wished she'd never reach his keep at all.

A devil living at the edge of the earth. A bastard son with white hair and one wife already dispatched in childbirth. She wondered how old he was. If he had white hair he was advanced in age, and if he was frail and old enough he couldn't pose her much harm, devil or not. She wondered what kind of home he lived in. A small cottage like the one she'd shared with Erma was easy to tend. If he was a bastard son and not well in the king's favor, he probably had a simple domicile, and she could try to live a simple life with him.

If he hated her, if he despised her for her looks or her personality or her parentage, well, she would bear it as well as she could. None of those were things she could change, any more than she could change this new path her life had taken.

* * * * *

The messenger arrived at Inverness Keep just before nightfall. He looked around the hall for the man they called the Devil. He hoped he wouldn't be overly angered by the news he was charged to impart. He was kept waiting some time as the earl was fetched from the practice fields and elected to bathe and take dinner before granting audience to his guest. When at last Lochlan was admitted before him, he worried that the subject of the message would arrive before the actual message did.

"My esteemed Lord Duncan, the king sends his greetings."

The Devil nodded, not looking up from his meal. Lochlan peered at him to be sure he was paying attention. Otherwise he was soon to be in for a surprise.

"Go on then, man, relay the message," Duncan prompted.

Chapter One

"I'm listening, but I'm a busy man and I must eat. Sit if you like and eat with us."

"Oh no, sir, thank you but—"

"The message then, quickly. What does the king require of me now?"

"The king wishes you to take a new wife."

Duncan laughed, taking a deep draft of his drink. "You may thank the king for his good wishes, friend, but I've less than no desire to be married again."

Lochlan hesitated, unsure of the best way to reveal the news.

"My lord, your new wife arrives presently. This very night. This hour perhaps."

Duncan paused, his face growing hard.

"What the hell did you say?"

The messenger swallowed, watching the Devil's hands curl into fists. He had expected a more sinister looking man, dark and strange like the bride they brought him. But the Devil earl was fair-haired with stormy grey eyes, as grey as the sea that surrounded the keep on three sides.

While he wasn't as dark and devilish looking as Lochlan expected, he was certainly angry. He feared the earl would toss him into that very sea before his message was fully told.

"The king has discovered a...lost daughter," Lochlan said delicately. "He finds her an...inconvenience at court, and wishes her to be married at once. To you, my lord," he added. "And she arrives this night."

Duncan sat a long time, his face darkening more with each passing moment.

"Connor, what do you make of this?" he finally murmured to the man on his right.

"I think you are about to become a bridegroom, my friend."

"I do not wish it. I would rather send her back."

The messenger raised his eyebrows in alarm. "My lord, the king commands—"

"Yes, the king commands me as he commands every Scotsman, but if he wants to know if I welcome his bastard as my wife, the answer is no. How old is she?"

"Uh, hmm...I know not exactly," said the messenger. "Of an age to be wed."

"Well, that's something. What else does the king request?"

"That is all, my lord. Just proof of a marriage to be conveyed back to him."

"Proof?" The Devil frowned. "What kind of proof?"

Lochlan blushed. "I believe a signed document will suffice. Have you a priest in your keep?"

"There is one in town proper." He nodded to his man, who stood and had some quick words with a servant by the door.

"And you will wait here for this document?"

"I am ordered to do so, my lord."

"Well," said Duncan, his lip curling distastefully. "We must all do as we are ordered, must we not?"

* * * * *

Duncan strode through the corridor cursing under his breath. His servants and men-at-arms all wisely stood clear. By God, he wanted to take somebody's head off. Again, a wife. His last one had nearly driven him insane.

Duncan was not a god-fearing man. In fact, there was very little in life that Duncan feared. By some cruel joke of the universe, or the king more like, he had found himself wed to the most insufferably religious shrew in Scotland. Judgmental, obsessive, ridiculously stupid. It was cruel of him, perhaps, to still regard her that way even after she'd died trying to bear his child. But Lenore had been a demon sent to torment him, perhaps from the devil himself.

She'd been beautiful enough on the outside—blonde like sunshine, with wide green eyes that sparkled like emeralds. She'd smiled at him the day of their marriage and been the most affable of brides until he'd taken her to his bed. From that moment she'd turned against him and nothing, nothing he did or said to her could have turned her back. It wasn't as if he'd been

Chapter One

cruel to her, as if he'd done anything that first night any man wouldn't have done to his wife. She called him *coarse*, and *lowborn*, and *degenerate*, any insult at all that she thought might keep him away. But he used her anyway, as any man would have, not even exposing her to his coarser desires.

Finally he managed to get her with child, and ceased performing his husbandly duties with her. Instead he found relief with the odd widow in the town only too happy to share herself for a bit of coin. Now, even that was taken from him. No woman would come near him with a moniker like *Devil* attached to his name. Attached forever to him, thanks to her and her shrewish screaming even in the throes of death.

She had died yowling and cursing him so the whole town could hear it. *Devil, you're the devil! Get away! Get away from me!* she'd shrieked with the last of her breath. *Black hearted, evil devil*! She had raved on and on as the last moments of her life bled away. He'd been nowhere near, but he'd heard her screams. He'd heard her accusations against him just as everyone else in the town had, and so now that was his name. *Devil.* Deserved or not. He had buried the baby boy and his wife the next morning with an honor and reverence he did not feel.

Devil. She didn't know the half of it. There was a side to him Lenore hadn't even seen, a side that would have sent her running home in hysterics to her father. Perhaps he should have shown it. Perhaps then she would still be alive.

He shoved thoughts of Lenore from his head and put his mind to his current problem. A bride, this night, and a priest on the way. A wedding to be performed and a document to be signed and delivered in good haste back to the king. He didn't want the king's oily messengers here any longer than they needed to be. He had a deep distrust of the king's court and all who moved in it.

This wife on the way to him raised his suspicions too. He'd not once heard even a whisper of a bastard daughter to the king. Perhaps that was by intention, which made him wonder who the mother was. He would question this daughter when she arrived, question her thoroughly before they wed. He would not be a party to any intrigue or strangeness. He was just a simple man who wanted to be left alone, who fulfilled his duties to the king and took good care of his townspeople. Yes, he would sit her down when she arrived and get to the bottom of things before he again took on the plague of a wife.

"Duncan," called Connor from the end of the corridor. "They've arrived. They are in the courtyard."

"Tell them to wait."

Duncan put on a fine black velvet surcoat. Pure vanity. But to meet a wife, even an unwanted one, a little vanity was allowed. He armed himself and strode back down the hall to the main entrance. He marched out the door as if going to battle and came to a sudden halt. His eyes swept the small assembly of rough-edged soldiers. He felt intense, inexplicable anger. Was his new wife so poorly regarded that she'd be sent across Scotland protected like this? He knew the low respect afforded to bastards, had lived with it his whole life, but it still provoked him to see it applied to someone who was to be his wife.

His stormy gaze swept over the small party and then back again. His anger was replaced by confusion. She wasn't even there. They hadn't even brought her as the messenger said.

But no, she was there. His eyes found her as one of the king's men helped her from her horse. She swayed on her legs as if she might collapse. He felt a sudden urge to run to her and steady her with his own hands. Her shoulders slumped and she was covered head to toe in grime and dust. A fit sight for a princess, even if she was a bastard one. If that could even possibly be her—she looked nothing at all like the king. But yes, perhaps in the shape of the eyes, the slant of the forehead. His gaze narrowed in distaste. Of an age to marry? If she was twelve years old he would be shocked. No matter. He had no intention of bedding her anyway. Not now, not ever.

"Bring her inside," he said brusquely before turning his back on her and walking away.

Chapter One

* * * * *

Cait tried to swallow the knot in her throat. She tried to will the tears from her eyes. She would not let him see her cry. She didn't want him to know how his cool dismissal hurt her. She let the king's soldier take her horse while she tried to find her land legs. No one else came to greet her in the gathering darkness.

And he was not old, no. He was not old at all, although white could certainly describe the pale blond color of his hair. He was quite young and strong, and hale enough to do her great harm if he wished it. From the look on his face, he wished it very much. He had scowled at her like he was the devil himself. She shuddered, remembering the coldness of his gaze.

He had looked at her in disbelief, as if she were so vile he could barely stand to look upon her, then turned from her and stalked away as if she meant nothing to him at all. She was unwanted by him just as she was unwanted by her father and everyone else.

At last an old woman came forward to herd her into the castle. So much for a cottage. The height of the great keep soared above her head, up over the banks of the firth, the pocked stone walls grey and bleak. The doors shut behind her with a crash and she blinked to adjust to the darkness.

She heard his voice just a few feet away.

"The priest comes soon, Henna. Clean the girl up as much as you can. And if you would," he added with barely veiled distaste, "be sure there are no lice."

Cait was pained by the indignity of her situation. She knew she must look a sight after days on the dusty roads with no bath.

"Yes, I will, my lord. Every girl should be clean when she's wed. What's your name, then, lass?" the old woman asked Cait. She was a plump, cheerful matron with a broad smiling face and small but friendly eyes. Cait tried to smile back at her.

"Caitlyn. Cait," she finally managed to say.

The woman nodded and patted her arm. "Her name is Caitlyn, my lord," she said loudly to the earl. "You can call her Cait as well, can't he, lass?"

"Yes, ma'am" she whispered, daring a glance up at the Devil. He looked strangely chastised by the old woman's tone.

"When *Caitlyn* is ready, bring her to the Great Hall," he said quietly.

Unwanted or not.

Chapter Two

"There now, lass," said the old woman as she huffed and puffed her bulk down the corridor next to Cait. "We'll get that dirt and grime off ya and have ya good as new for your wedding. It won't do at all to get married when you're a mess, now will it?"

"No, ma'am," said Cait tiredly. What she really wanted to do was find a nice warm bed to sleep in and call it a night.

Henna led her to a small room off the kitchen. Cait wandered through the hustle and bustle of servants and cooks and children, feeling dazed by all the activity. The keep, while large and forbidding, was also teeming with life. The smells of delicious food wafted in the air, making her stomach growl loudly enough for the old woman to hear.

"Oh now, we'll have some food for you too, lass. You're hungry, aren't you? Had dinner yet?"

"No, ma'am," said Cait. "I'm awfully hungry. I'm sorry to trouble you."

"Sorry for what? We feed hungry mouths here. The earl insists on it," she laughed. "Now what would you like to tide you over to dinner? Bit o' bread or cheese, or maybe a fresh apple?"

"Some bread would be good. And something to drink too, if it's not too much trouble."

"Oh, I'm sure you're parched. Where's my manners? I'll set them to warming the water and let you eat while you soak in the tub. Go on. Go on, I'll help ya."

She pushed Cait into a small room. She stood aside as an army of servants came in carrying buckets of hot water to pour into a large tub in the corner. Cait eyed it in wonder. It was made for a giant. For *him*, she supposed.

Henna returned with a large mug of fresh ale and a plate of bread, fruit, and cheese. Cait drained the mug and tried not to eat too eagerly. It was hard though. She was so hungry.

"Take your time, girl," said the old woman. "You can eat 'til you're full. There's plenty more than that if you want it. You'll need your energy for tonight, won't ya, lass?" she said with a mischievous wink.

Cait looked back at her in confusion. "I suppose."

"Well, then, let's get those filthy things off ya. Have you any other clothes to put on?"

"No, ma'am," said Cait. "Nothing any cleaner than this."

"That won't do." The old woman frowned. "Let Henna take care of this. You climb into that water and wash yourself good, and I'll be back to help with your hair in just a bit."

Cait looked at the warm, steaming tub and then back at the door. The kitchen was so near. What if someone saw her? She decided finally that she didn't care. She peeled off the filthy clothes of the last two weeks and left them in a pile. She stepped into the water and sighed. It was so warm, so warm.

* * * * *

By the time Henna returned a few minutes later, Cait was reclining in the tub, fast asleep. Henna looked down at the exhausted girl. Poor thing, little more than a child, and no idea at all what she'd gotten herself into. She was certain the girl knew

Chapter Two

nothing of men or what happened on wedding nights, if her blank look earlier meant anything. She wished she could allow her to rest now, but she had to get her washed up and delivered to the earl.

She roused her gently and began to wash the grit and dust from her dark hair. Jet black, she thought to herself as the chalky dirt washed away. Never seen hair so jet black. Black as the devil it was. And the eyes, when the girl turned them on her, they took her breath away. They were otherworldly. So light, so blue.

"Are you scared about tonight, lass?" she asked as she washed out the long wavy locks, rinsing them over and over until they shone like ebony stone.

"Yes," she said, "but I think this bath is worth it, even if I must be wed to a stranger."

Henna laughed. "You can have a bath every night if you wish. That's what the earl does. Had this wash room made special, he did, when the old king gave him this keep."

"He gave it to him?"

"Aye," said Henna proudly. "For valor in battle."

She gave the girl scented cakes of soap, helping her wash her back. She was so thin and tired. Henna couldn't wait to get some meat on her bones and fill her out a little. She'd be a pretty thing when she was in full health, not that she wasn't pretty now. For a thin woman, she had lovely curves, full breasts and adequate hips for bearing babes. Henna knew such things. She'd helped birth the earl and his brother, God rest his soul, and nursed them both from the day they were born.

"Is he the fighting sort then?" asked the girl. "Is he very vicious?"

Henna laughed out loud. "Vicious? Oh, goodness me no, although he can have a temper when he wants. Don't you believe for a second that he's the devil they say. He's a fine man and he'll treat you all right. Otherwise he'll have me to answer to."

The girl looked up at her and smiled. "Are you his mother?"

"No, dear, his mother passed a while back. But I was his nurse for many years. I take care of him still, although he would never admit it."

The girl laughed. Henna smiled at the tinkly, light sound of it, but just as quickly the girl's face grew sober.

"I think he doesn't like me very much. He didn't look happy to see me."

"You must understand that he only learned you were coming a short time before you arrived. And his last wife..." Henna's voice trailed off.

"His last wife died, didn't she?"

"Yes, she died. During childbirth. Just a matter of how the baby came out. I wish I could have helped her, but her problems were the unfixable kind."

Henna waited for more questions but they never came. She helped the girl out of the water and dried her off. She was a little thing, she was. All woman, but short and tiny-like.

"Are you worried about after the wedding, lass, you know?" she asked, not wanting to volunteer any information that might scare the girl.

"I'm just tired," Cait replied after a moment. "I'm just so very tired. I can't wait to go to bed."

* * * * *

Connor nudged Duncan as Henna led his bride into the hall. By God, he recognized the dress at once, but the girl wearing it, that was something else altogether. Gone was the dust covered urchin of the courtyard, replaced by an astonishingly beautiful woman.

And she *was* a woman, not a child at all. Lenore's dress revealed that, even swimming in it as she was. Lenore had been taller, so the material pooled at her feet, but the bust and hips of the dress were filled out by delicious curves.

But no, it wouldn't do for her to wear this dress. Not tonight. Lenore was in his memory enough as it was. He shot a reproachful look at Henna, beckoning her to his side.

"It was the only dress that was suitable—" she insisted.

"It is not suitable. It belonged to my dead wife."

"The dress does not matter," Henna argued under her breath. "What matters is the woman inside it."

"The dress does matter!"

"Why?" asked Henna.

Because I hated her. Because she made me miserable. Because she died. "Because I say so. She cannot wear Lenore's dress for this ceremony. Find her another. I don't care if it's yours, or the laundress's, or the cook's, as long as it's not Lenore's."

"She needs a fine dress for the wedding!"

"Henna, you know I love you well but do not test me on this. Find her another. I order it. Now."

He looked over at the girl. Caitlyn. *Cait.* She watched them arguing with an anxious look on her face. As if she had not been through enough, he thought. Now he would make her be married in a washerwoman's dress.

Henna led her from the hall and Cait let herself be dragged along without complaint. He could see she was tired, absolutely exhausted. He put his head in his hands and rubbed his eyes. His friend Connor chuckled.

"Duncan, it's not the end of the world, man. She's half a comely thing anyway, isn't she though? If you've got to take a wife, it's nice to have a pretty one to look at."

"Lenore was a pretty wife," Duncan replied.

"Ah, well," Connor sighed.

Duncan sat and sipped from his goblet, trying to school his face from the misery he felt. It was one thing to revile taking a wife, but quite another to announce it to his townspeople by the expression on his face. As he expected, Henna took her time finding a new gown for his young bride, but he didn't care. The priest was happily getting drunk in the corner with the king's men, and the crowd was enjoying themselves, getting rowdier and rowdier as they waited for the festivities to begin.

Finally, at long last, his bride reappeared. The dress was passable. It would do. A townswoman's dress, he guessed.

Whoever it was would have been honored to lend it to his bride. He stood and approached her, studying her as he came nearer. Her hair was so black, so long, and gone completely to wild curls. Her body, as he'd already noted, was too appealing by far. But her eyes surprised him most. They were so light, almost transparent. The thorough questioning he'd planned suddenly seemed unnecessary. Those eyes could hide nothing from him.

"Hello," he said, because he had no idea what else to say to her.

"Hello." She spoke so softly that he barely heard her. She dipped down into a curtsy, bowing her head. He drew in his breath.

Damn it, she was so beautiful. That was really going to complicate things. That was really going to make his life a lot more bloody unbearable than it already was. He frowned deeply, and at the forbidding look on his face, she looked away, suddenly afraid.

And that fear, it both troubled and aroused him. Complicated? No, this was going to be worse than complicated. It would be a bloody mess. He'd been standing next to her for less than a minute and already he felt feelings he'd shoved deep down inside him shuddering back to life. Her vulnerability, her fear response, the sexual pull of her body...damn it.

He took a deep breath and grabbed her hand. So much for talking. It was time to do the king's duty. Get married to her so the priest would sign the paper and he could pawn her off on Henna and not set eyes on her again. For her own good, and for his too.

The priest was mercifully quick. Even holding her hand was excruciating, the way it curled so trustingly in his and yet trembled at the same time. He said his vows but thought the whole time of what she'd look like stripped naked to his gaze. For her part, she spoke the vows true and clear, although she was obviously shy. Her voice sounded light like bells and her lips were so shapely, so luscious. He watched them avidly, picturing them wrapped around his—

Chapter Two

No, he wasn't going to do it. He wasn't even going to try it. He would just end up reviled by another woman, labeled Devil again. She was far too innocent anyway, that much was plain. If she even realized men had cocks between their legs he'd be surprised. More likely she'd cry and plead for mercy as Lenore had when she'd seen him the first time and realized what he meant to do to her, what all men did to their wives.

Well, no matter. He could take care of his own needs, and he would. Probably fifty times in a row before he put out the fire she'd lit. As soon as the priest blessed them, he dropped her hand like it burned him and beckoned Henna to his side.

"She's tired. Put her to bed in the room adjoining mine."

"But my lord—"

"Henna, no argument please. Just for tonight. I'll consummate this farce of a marriage when I see fit. Set her up in the adjoining room. And tell her to lock the door."

Henna's reproachful look irked him, but better to bear her disapproval than to plow his wife tonight. He might do it eventually, against his better judgment, but he would do it when his desires were under better control. If he had her now, he would do things to her they would both regret. He couldn't bear to see again that same condemnation he'd seen in Lenore's eyes.

"Good night, wife," he said curtly, giving her a quick peck on the cheek. He would follow soon after and let everyone believe he went to her. He strode to Lochlan carrying the certificate of marriage for the king. Appearances were everything in situations like these.

* * * * *

Sleep at last. Cait was too tired to figure out why Henna was so agitated. She blustered and clucked and muttered under her breath, but Cait only wanted to sleep.

"I'm sure he'll come to you tomorrow, lass. Don't you worry." She helped her change into a filmy sleeping shift. The thing was so fine and soft, it amazed her. All these fine clothes and furnishings, they were nothing like what she and Erma had in their little cottage. Everything was different now. She lived in a castle on the water, and she was married to a powerful man, and now she was going to bed on a soft mattress covered in fine linens, not the simple cot she'd slept on next to Erma in the middle of the woods.

She slid between the soft sheets and pulled the blankets up to her ears. She felt like a new woman in a world of new sensations. The softness of the bed, the silkiness of the shift, the hardness of his body when she'd brushed against it. The roughness of his face when he'd kissed her cheek. The solid firmness of his lips. She'd never in her life stood so close to a man, never rested her hand in one's rough grasp. She'd never been kissed. She hadn't thought she would like it, but she liked it very much.

She felt strangely emotional in her exhaustion. She wanted to cry. She wanted to smile. She wanted to have the earl's attention. She wanted him to like her, not glare at her and dismiss her. More than all that, she wanted to look at him some more, because it pleased her so much to look at him. It pleased her too much. It excited her. It made her heart beat hard.

She hated to admit it, how handsome and appealing she found him. His hand on hers had been strong and reassuring. If only he didn't sigh and frown so much, she might have been able to at least pretend he liked her.

No matter. There was nothing to be done about it. She supposed these arranged marriages happened all the time. Husbands and wives made the best of them and learned to live with each other. Maybe someday, if she was sweet and charming enough, he would be able to see past her faults and appearance and find a way to bear being near her. Maybe tomorrow when she was rested, when she didn't look so tired and stumble over her words, he would find her more appealing as a wife.

"Henna," she asked in the darkened room. "Will I see him tomorrow?"

"Of course you will. He's your husband now. He'll be about.

Chapter Two

And he sleeps right there, over in the next room beside yours."

"What can a wife do, Henna, to make her husband glad?"

Henna frowned. "Well, I'm sure he's glad of ya, Caitlyn. He's just...he's getting used to being married again. You don't take it to mean he's not concerned for your well being, because I'm sure he is. He'll be a good husband to you."

"Only because he has to," whispered Cait.

"Oh, lass. When you get to know him and he gets to know you, things will be different. Mark my words. You may not find love with each other, but if you respect one another you'll live happily. I see already you care for his happiness. He's a lucky man for that."

"I don't know if I'll be able to make him happy. I think I'm not pretty enough, and not what he wanted."

"Oh, now, you don't talk that way. You're a lovely girl, and well mannered and sweet, with those childbearing hips that men prefer. You don't go worrying your pretty head about these matters tonight. It takes time for a marriage to take shape. Time and patience and understanding. And respect."

"Will he ever love me, Henna? Do you think?" she asked wistfully. She didn't know why she was being so silly and sentimental. She supposed it was because his eyes were so unbelievably beautiful and deep.

"I hope he will, sweet. If you want love, I hope you find it. Both of ya together. It happens more often than you think. Now close your eyes and rest. You're plumb exhausted. It's late and the castle will be up and astir as soon as the sun rises in the sky. Rest and sleep now. You're safe in your husband's castle. Tomorrow's a new day, with new experiences to come."

She stroked Cait's hair in a motherly fashion, and tears came to her eyes from remembering Erma doing the same.

"Henna, thank you," she murmured sleepily.

"I'm here to be a help to ya, lass. Whatever you need, you let Mama Henna know, and I'll do what I can."

Can you make him fall in love with me, Henna? I think that's what I'd really like.

And with that thought, her eyes closed and she dreamed of pale grey eyes and strong capable hands, and the feeling of one day nestling in his welcoming arms.

* * * * *

Damn it. Of course sleep would be impossible. She was so close to him, so near. He swore he could smell the fetching scent of her skin through the stone wall. God, it was insufferable. Why hadn't he just availed himself of her? She was his now anyway, no man could say she was not.

He sighed heavily and took his cock in hand again, stroking it, soothing it. As he'd expected, self-abuse took none of the yearning away.

He remembered the curve of her neck and back as she'd bowed before him. How he longed to put his hands on that graceful neck and tilt her head back, baring her throat to his touch, his lick, his bite. He wanted to strip her naked and lick every godforsaken inch of her. Lay her down and run his hands over her pillowy breasts, her supple thighs. He hadn't even seen her goddamn thighs yet, but he knew they were perfect just like the rest of her. He would have given anything, anything at all just to walk through the door to her room and bare those thighs to his gaze. But then he'd have to put his hands on them, and he'd spread them wide and—

Enough. He remembered the blood, the screaming, the accusations as Lenore lay dying. Did he really want to risk that again, especially with a treasure like Caitlyn? He was a bastard. It made no difference if he had an heir or not. The attraction to her would wear off. It had to, with time and exposure and a concerted effort not to be near her, not to touch her or look in her beguiling eyes. He would assign keepers to her and let her go where she wanted, do what she wanted, see who she wanted, as long as she left him alone.

And Henna would look after her too. She had already taken the girl firmly under her wing. It would be fine. He would just

Chapter Two

avoid her until he sorted out what to do, how to deal with her, how to keep his vile desires from ruining her life. He was a strong man. He could bear anything. As long as he didn't see her naked. By God, as long as he wasn't inflicted with that. As long as he didn't have to see the curve of her hips tapering down to her delicately round...God help him.

He imagined for the hundredth time pulling her over his lap to run his hands over her shapely bottom. Rubbing it, cupping it, parting the cheeks to caress her and make her moan. Landing a sharp smack, watching her jump, feeling her twist against him. His cock was rock hard again. He took it in his hand with a sigh. How he would love to belabor her beautiful bottom, make it scarlet and sore, and then pull her up in his arms and soothe her, make it all better by impaling her on his cock—ah—

Masturbation was getting him nowhere. Even after the climax, the desire was still there. He turned on his side, determined to salvage what he could of the night, determined to sleep.

Determined to forget about the girl who'd stoked such dangerous fires back to life.

Chapter Three

Cait slept long, long past morning. When she awakened she had
no idea what time it was, only that the sun was high in the sky.
She had nothing to wear aside from the sheer shift. In fact there
was nothing in the room she occupied except for the bed she lay
on and a wooden chair beside it.

She remembered then what Henna had told her the night
before, that the earl slept in the room adjoining hers. She pulled a
blanket around her shoulders and crept over to the door in the
wall and put her ear to it. She heard no sound. She unlocked it,
trying not to make any noise. Slowly she opened the door until
there was a small crack to peek through. She saw his massive
bed, rumpled and unmade, but he wasn't in it.

Of course, he was not the sort of man to lie in bed all day.
He'd probably been up at dawn working, fighting, whatever the
king's earls did. She spun as the door to her own room opened
and Henna bustled in. Cait guiltily shut the door to the earl's
room and leaned back against it.

Henna laughed. "Oh lass, you look like the cat that stole the buttermilk. Take a look if it pleases ya. He's not there."

"Where is he?"

"Down on the practice fields, I gather, or meeting with his men in the hall. Take a look. He has nothing to hide from you."

"What if he catches me? He'll be angry."

"Of course he won't. He's your husband."

"I better not," she said, even though she really wanted to go in and lie in his bed and breathe in the smell of him.

"Well, I've brought you some breakfast," Henna said, laying a heavily laden tray on the chair beside Cait's bed. "And I've set the seamstress to sewing a gown for you too. It should be done shortly. Something simple to keep you warm until you choose fabric for more fashionable dresses. The earl will want you to have several pretty gowns, I'm sure."

"Will he?" Cait was skeptical. She sat on the bed and picked at the tray. The fresh bread and milk looked and smelled wonderful, but she didn't feel like eating.

"Go on, now," Henna urged. "You're far too thin. I'll be unhappy if you don't eat it, lass."

Slowly, Cait forced herself to eat. She would have given anything for this warm, delicious food on the journey here, but now it didn't appeal to her. She wondered when she would see the earl again.

"May I walk around the grounds, around the castle?" asked Cait.

"You certainly may. The earl wishes for you to have a guard at all times though. You can't go wandering around alone, being his wife and the king's daughter."

"Why? Am I in danger?"

"Oh of course not, lass, but you can never be too careful. Someone has a tiff with the king, or an itch to ransom the wife of the Earl of Inverness, you know how it is."

"Ransom? I never thought of such a thing."

"Well, there's bandits about who'll think of almost anything to gain some coin by ill means. You shouldn't forget that. Just stay by your guard and you'll be perfectly safe. You're to be allowed to go wherever you wish as long as you don't go by yourself."

"Oh," said Cait. "I guess I can do that."

After breakfast Cait's new gown still wasn't ready, so she put on the gown from the day before and decided to wander around. Her guard, a young soldier named Mitchum, looked as if he'd rather be anywhere else than tagging along after her. But duty was duty, she supposed, and if the earl wanted him to follow her around, it wasn't her fault. She explored every inch of the castle from top to bottom, strolled around the grounds, and even ventured a short distance into the town.

She walked everywhere and looked everywhere but not once did she manage to catch sight of the man she wanted to see. *Him.* The Devil. Her husband.

She might have asked Mitchum where he was if she wasn't so embarrassed, and if he didn't have such an annoyed frown on his face. She would have asked Henna, but she kept so busy with the running of the castle all day that Cait was loathe to disturb her. She wished she would just run into him. She didn't know why she wanted to see him so much. She was curious, that was all. And lonely. And she wanted him to touch her hand again.

But no, she saw him nowhere. For all she knew, he might have ridden off to another town for the day or the week or...God, she hoped not...the month. Dejected, she returned to the castle. Her guard dropped her off with relief at her room. Again, skittishly, she cracked open the door to his bedroom but no, no sign of him there.

After a moment's hesitation she slipped into the silent room, shutting the door behind her. It was much larger than her room, which made sense because he was so much larger than she. It was not much more furnished though. The large bed, a couple of chairs, a chest in the corner. A couple of weapons leaning against the wall she was afraid to touch, although she looked at them closely, frightening as they were.

Against her better judgment, she went to his bed and crawled into it, not worrying overmuch about jostling the bedding since

Chapter Three

he apparently never made his bed. The sheets were tangled in a ball. How he must toss and turn in his sleep! She smoothed them out carefully. If he caught her now she could just claim she was straightening his room. Wasn't that something any good wife would do? She ran her hand across the pillow, then lay down to rest her cheek upon it. It smelled clean and bracing and yes, it smelled of him. She breathed in and out, long and slow. Perhaps she would just lie here a minute and rest. He wouldn't be coming anytime soon. What would it hurt, anyway? She was his wife after all.

* * * * *

Henna bustled down the hall carrying Cait's gown in her arms, and a warmer shift for sleeping that she hoped would please her.

"Good afternoon, Mitchum lad," she said to the surly soldier sitting in a chair outside her room. "What are ya doing? Surely the earl doesn't expect you to wait here at her door?"

"Yes, ma'am, he does. He says when you're not with her, I'm to be, and wherever she is I'm to be there too."

"Well, no one's going to snatch her from her own bedroom, I gather. But I suppose you must listen to your lord."

"Yes, ma'am," he said. He was glad he had only one day of this duty a week. Following a girl around was a hell of a job for a soldier like him. The other men would be snickering behind their hands at him if they could see him sitting outside her door like some blasted lady in waiting.

"Oh, now, it wasn't that difficult, was it?" chided Henna. "Was the lass such a trial to you? Such a frown!"

"No, she wasn't any trouble, but she did run all over the place, and the earl gave me strict orders to—"

"To what?" prompted Henna suspiciously.

"To be sure she stayed out of his way," said Mitchum. "He said to keep her out of his sight as much as I could."

"Really?" said Henna, her eyes narrowing. "He said that, did he? I wonder why. Well." She would have a talk with him about that. What a thing to say about his new wife, and to her guard no less. It was absolutely churlish.

"Do you think she's sleeping?" Henna asked. "How long has she been within?"

"An hour at least, perhaps more."

Henna knocked softly. There was no answer. She opened the door a crack to peek inside, then swung it open, looking all around. "She's not here! She's not here at all, Mitchum! You've lost her already!"

"Oh, holy God," he said, leaping to his feet.

* * * * *

Duncan was going to kill that boy Mitchum. How difficult could it be to keep track of one mousy girl? He would deal with him later. For now, he had soldiers searching the castle grounds for Cait while he combed the woods around the keep. For God's sake, he had plenty of important work to be doing besides looking for her. He tried to convince himself his agitated state was only frustration, but in truth his heart was hammering anxiously in his chest. He had enemies and so did the king, and there were bandits in the woods around Inverness just as there were bandits everywhere. The idea of someone taking her, of her in fright, in peril... He couldn't stand it.

He nudged his horse to a gallop and took off in the other direction. His men met him in a clearing.

"Nothing. No sign of her, Lord Duncan. But she couldn't have gone far. Mitchum said he'd seen her an hour before—"

"Mitchum is an idiot who's not to be trusted. No sign of her in town?"

"Perhaps we should search the castle proper again. Check in some of the unused rooms," suggested Connor. "She could be hiding."

Duncan scowled at him. "Hiding? What the hell for? What are you trying to say?"

Chapter Three

"I'm not trying to say anything," Connor hedged. "But many a bride wakes up from her wedding night confused and upset."

"Not my bride. She has no reason to be hiding. Believe me."

Still, the men wheeled their mounts around to return to the keep. Forget about Mitchum, thought Duncan. When he got hold of *her*, he was going to let her know exactly and in no uncertain terms what running away and hiding from him resulted in, and it would be very difficult for her to sit down after that lesson had been taught.

"Any sign of her?" he asked Henna when he entered the courtyard.

"No, my lord. Oh, dear, where could she have gone?"

"You spoke to her this morning? What was her demeanor?"

"Oh, she was just normal. I don't know. She had little appetite, but I'd no thought she would go running off. I don't think she's run off at all! I think someone's taken her!"

"From the third floor of the keep? I doubt it. She's hiding. I want her found."

He strode into the hall and up the stone stairs, Henna tripping at his heels.

"What will ya do to her when you find her? You must be gentle with her. She never asked to come here and be your bride—"

"Silence!" he said. "I will deal with my wife as I choose."

He took the stairs two at a time, leaving Henna behind him, and barged into his room to pick up the weapons he'd left behind. He was halfway back to the door when he stopped short, staring in disbelief.

The lass every man in the castle was searching for was fast asleep on his bed.

Not just *on* his bed. The blasted wench was *in* it, snuggled right under his blankets making herself at home. He strode to the door and yelled down the hall.

"Did *no one* think to check my room? Call off the blasted search, you sorry lot of idiots!"

He slammed the door and turned on Cait, who was now very

much awake. She inched from the bed, hopped down to the floor, and at the look on his face, sidled around to the other side.

"What were you doing in here?" The quiet, controlled tone of his voice belied the anger bubbling beneath.

"I—I fell asleep. I'm sorry. I didn't mean to."

"You have your own room. Your own bed to sleep in," he reminded her tightly. "I'll ask you once again. What were you doing in here?"

"I just...I came in to look...to see if you were here. I hadn't seen you all day."

"There is a reason for that. I'm a very busy man, and I don't have time to act as playmate to my wife. If you wish for company you can look for it elsewhere. I'm sure the women of the keep will be happy to comply."

"Oh," she murmured miserably.

"My men have been combing the woods for you for an hour. They have been over every inch of the castle and grounds in search of you—"

"I was right here!"

"Don't interrupt me," he snapped, "or things will go very badly for you. I assigned a guard to you so I would know at all times that you are safe. He is now in grave dishonor because of your capricious behavior. I don't care what you decide to do, but from now on, if you leave your room your guard is to know exactly where you are. Do you understand me?"

"But, sir—"

"Do you understand?" he barked.

She bowed her head. "Yes."

"Repeat it to me."

"I'm to make sure my guard knows where I am at all times. Whenever I leave my room," she whispered.

"Furthermore, you will remember that this is my room. *My* room. You are not permitted in my room, and certainly not in my bed. From now on you are not to set foot in this room no matter how much you wish to know if I am here. Do you understand?"

"Yes sir," she said, her eyes filling with tears.

Chapter Three

Tears. She wouldn't sway him with those tears. He pressed on, angrier at himself than with her. He had to hurt her. He had to make her see that for her own good, she had to leave him alone.

"And listen to me now, little Cait. You may be the king's own daughter, but you will not be permitted to do whatever you please. If I find you in this room again, you will be punished. Severely punished. And I promise you, if you ever go missing again through your own carelessness, if you ever leave your guard without an idea of your whereabouts, you will rue the day you were born. Do you understand me?"

"Yes sir." She swiped away the tears as they fell. Tears like little diamonds. He wished he could catch every one of them and put them back from whence they came. It was for her own good, *her own good.* He would punish her if she couldn't abide by his rules. They were for her. He tried to convince himself of that as he pointed to her door and watched her slink out of his room.

Henna shut the door behind her, shooting him a reproachful look. Of course she had listened to every word of his harangue. She would rake him over the coals for it later. So be it. He could handle Henna much more easily than the other one, the beautiful, lonely, needy one with the pale blue eyes.

He sat on the edge of the bed, tried not to remember how charming she looked curled up in the middle of his bed. Her arms had been wrapped about his pillow as if she embraced it. As if she embraced him. He imagined embracing her, taking her in his arms, parting her legs and plunging deep inside—

Gods, it was farcical. Not only was she innocent as a newborn, she also obviously had no inkling of what went on in the marriage bed. But maybe...maybe he could use that to his advantage. How was she to know that the things he wanted to demand of her were not what every man demanded of his wife?

No. She would instinctively know his requests were unnatural, just as Lenore had known even though she'd been virginal as a nun when she came to him. Women knew. He couldn't bear to have those innocent, beautiful eyes turn on him in condemnation. Better to leave things as they were. Her tears would dry. Life would go on, somehow, some way. But God, if he wasn't a miserable fool.

* * * * *

Caitlyn was absent from the dinner table, and while Duncan wasn't surprised, he wasn't exactly relieved either. He had hoped to see her at dinner if only to reassure himself that her tears were gone, that she was all right. That she was coming to accept the way things needed to be between them.

Henna was only too happy to inform him of Cait's demeanor as soon as she caught him alone, and her report wasn't good.

"She cried for two hours, lad. I hope you're happy with yourself. I don't think I've ever seen such a loving display of husbandly care and concern."

"Henna, please, I've just eaten. Be so kind as to not ruin my digestion."

"You ruined hers! She's so upset and hurt I couldn't get her to eat one bite. What is this game you're playing with her?"

"No game. I won't coddle the girl. She can't be expecting me to hold her hand all day and sing love poems to her and play pat-a-cake."

"Oh, please, you don't fool me for a second. This has nothing to do with her, and everything to do with Lenore—"

"Don't." His face grew hard. "Don't, Henna."

"Well, it's not fair to her. It's not. I can tell already this girl is nothing like Lenore. Nothing, and yet you treat her as if—"

"I treat her as if she's an unwanted infringement on my time and patience, which she is."

"How cold you are. The lass is lonely and confused. All she wants from you is a smile, a kiss on the cheek, some indication that you don't despise her. Did you really tell her guard to keep her away from ya? How rude, how perfectly horrid for a husband to behave!"

"You don't understand."

Chapter Three

"How much effort does it take to give your wife's hand a squeeze? To smile at her once, just one time a day to greet her and say hello? And how do you expect her to perform her wifely duties when you're so cold to her—"

"I don't," he snapped. "I don't expect her to. I don't want her to."

Henna drew back in surprise. "You'll profane your own marriage and hers—"

"I'll not take a child like her to my bed. She's a girl, an innocent. Another virgin who'll cry and complain at the first taste of marital play."

"She's not a girl." Henna huffed indignantly. "She's a woman and she pines for you. She's been made wife to a husband who pushes her away, and she's rightfully confused about it. She looks for you and asks all day where you are, when you'll see her again."

"That will all change if I take her to my bed. Anyway, I have no desire to bury another wife."

Henna paused, understanding dawning over her face. Her expression turned sympathetic.

"Oh, lad. Is that what this is all about then?"

"No, it's not. Henna, believe me, it's much more complicated than you can comprehend. But I don't have to explain my behavior to you, or to anyone, as far as it regards my wife. I'll thank you to remember that."

"You know it's only because I love you, lad. I do. I love you like my own son."

"I know. I love you too, but I'll not support this meddling. If it continues, I'll find Caitlyn another attendant and forbid you to see her. She'll learn soon enough her proper place here. She'll learn to live with things as they are, if you don't complicate matters."

Henna bowed her head, wisely deciding to bite her tongue, but as she walked away she muttered under her breath, "It's not me that's complicating things, Duncan dear."

Cait and the Devil

Cait lay awake in bed long past sunset, her eyes too sore from crying to sleep. She didn't know why his rejection smarted so much. It's not as if she wasn't coming to expect it in recent days. She didn't understand what it was about her that so offended him. Was she so repellent, that he couldn't even stand her in his bed, in his room? He acted as if she profaned it with her mere presence. She wanted to beg him to tell her what was wrong with her, to tell her what she could change.

But she didn't. She couldn't, so she only cried until she was so sore and tired she couldn't cry any more. Even then, she couldn't sleep. She just kept replaying the wretched conversation over and over in her mind.

If I find you in this room again, you will be punished. Severely punished.

His hands had made fists when he said that, and she knew he meant he would hurt her with his hands. He would beat her, just as all men beat women who weren't obedient to their demands.

If you ever leave your guard without an idea of your whereabouts, you will rue the day you were born.

He was so big, so strong. It would hurt terribly if he rained blows on her in anger. Still, at least then he would be touching her. At least then he would take notice of her. She thought, somehow, it would be better than this grief.

Chapter Four

Oh, she was an imp. She really was. If she was testing him, she was about to reap the very real rewards of such folly.

She'd eluded her guard again, but this time he'd seen the entire thing unfold from his vantage point on the upper practice field. He watched her hurry for the orchard, looking back over her shoulder.

"Ian, I'll return in a while. I leave you in charge. When Desmond arrives to report my wife missing, relieve him of his duty for the day without prejudice."

"Yes sir," Ian said, barely disguising his puzzlement.

Duncan mounted his horse and wheeled towards the orchard, knowing exactly which tree she'd crawled into. He'd promised her punishment the next time she evaded her guard. So be it.

When he reached the tree he dismounted. He approached the leafy apple tree and looked up through the branches to find Caitlyn balancing on a bough near the top.

"Come down," he said sharply. "If that branch breaks and you fall—"

"It won't matter, will it? You don't want me anyway. If you're lucky I'll break my neck."

"Caitlyn. Come down. Right now."

"No," she yelled.

He stared up at her in surprise. Her chin jutted out and she pouted down at him. His little mouse was not so mousy after all.

"Caitlyn, either way you'll be punished just as I promised you. If I have to drag you down, it will go worse, much worse."

He watched her consider that. Fear and anxiety clouded her expression for a moment, and then she turned churlish again.

"Why do you care if I leave my guard, anyway? If you value me so little?"

He sighed heavily. He'd like to climb up in the tree and shake some sense into the little twit, but the branches were barely strong enough to support her, much less his massive bulk.

"I value you as much as any man values his wife."

"Which is not at all."

"Whether I value you or not is not the issue here. You were told not to wander off alone. You were warned that you would be punished if you did. I know you don't know me very well, but I'm a man of my word and I do what I say. You will be punished before we leave this orchard."

"Punished how?" she asked, a slight tremor in her voice.

Good, she was listening.

"I'm going to bend you over my lap and spank your bottom until it hurts you to sit down. Hopefully that will teach you how important it is to obey my commands."

"Well," she said after a moment. "In that case, I'm never coming down."

Duncan stifled a smile. It really wasn't funny. He shouldn't have been laughing, but the cowed expression on her face, the resolve in her voice... She truly believed if she just sat in the tree long enough that he'd give up and go away. He crossed his arms over his chest and schooled his face to a stern glare.

"I promise you I can wait here an awfully long time, Cait. All night if I must."

Chapter Four

She didn't answer. He peered up to find her biting into an apple and gazing down at him with a baleful expression.

He sucked in a breath. God, she plagued him. But he wanted her. He wanted her so badly he ached. He was actually enjoying having her trapped in the tree at his mercy. He might keep her there all night only to look up at her expressive blue eyes and her red pouting mouth. He watched her lick apple juice from her lips.

"Caitlyn," he called up. "Throw me down an apple too, if you will. And one for my horse."

"Okay," she said after a moment, wiping her mouth on her sleeve and her hands on her skirts. She looked around the fruit laden branches and selected a nice, ripe, shiny one. She tossed it down to him. He'd expected her to find the wormiest, most pocked one in the tree, but no, not Caitlyn. She threw down another for his horse and he caught it, strolling over to feed his stallion the treat. When he returned, he found her looking down for him anxiously.

"I'm still here," he reassured her.

It touched him, how she sought him. She seemed to need him so desperately. Why? Why was his presence, his approval so important to her when he was only standing down here to dole out a punishment?

And what on earth was he going to do with the girl? It became more obvious with each passing moment that she was elementally attractive to him. He looked down at the ground, frowning, then up at her again. He still held the apple, perfect and red, cradled in his hand.

"Aren't you hungry?" she asked.

"No, I'm not hungry, Cait. I'm frustrated. I'm tired of waiting down here for you. I want you to come down before that branch breaks."

"If I come down, will you still punish me?"

"Yes, I'm going to punish you. I'm growing more irritated by the moment, as a matter of fact."

"That's why I don't want to come down."

"Well, you should have considered the consequences before you tested me."

"I wish you would just hold me instead."

Her soft, wistfully spoken words took him aback. He bit into the apple, chewing slowly and thinking over what she'd just said.

"Cait—"

"I wish you wanted me," she said. "Because I wish you would hold me. I would like that much better than...being punished."

He sighed. He would have to put his hands on her sooner or later. He was only delaying the inevitable as it was.

"Listen, Caitlyn. If you'll come down at once and submit to the punishment you earned, then afterward, I'll hold you as you wish."

She looked down at him, considering, the corners of her mouth drawn down in the most charming little frown.

"And I caution you, I'm not normally one to bargain, especially not in situations like this. However, your honesty and openness has moved me. You have thirty seconds to decide what to do. After that my offer to hold you is withdrawn."

It was her turn to sigh. She looked down at him warily.

"How much will it hurt?"

"It's a punishment, Cait. It's not going to feel good."

"How long will it last?"

"No more questions. Enough. Make your decision. Just remember, your punishment comes either way, so the best choice should be obvious. You have ten seconds left to decide."

With another soft sigh, she threw down her apple core and began to ease herself from the crook of the branch.

"Be careful. Come slowly." He instinctively positioned himself below her in case she should fall. When she was in arm's reach of him, he took her waist in his hands and lifted her to the ground. Her arms came around his shoulders for balance and her face leaned close to his. He could smell the sweetness of apple on her lips, on her sticky hands.

Reluctantly she met his gaze. "I'm sorry," she said, fighting back tears. "I'm not usually so bad."

"Aren't you, Cait?" he replied skeptically.

"Well," she whispered, "I don't want to be. I don't want you to punish me."

He watched her hands as they clasped and unclasped in front of her. She looked up at him mournfully.

"I just want you to...to like me. I don't want you to be unhappy with me."

Two fat tears rolled down her cheeks and she stared at his hands while she sniffled under his gaze.

"It will make me happy if you obey me, Cait. And if you submit gracefully to punishment when you don't. No more climbing up in trees to delay the inevitable."

She stole another anxious glance into his eyes, to find them sympathetic and kind.

"I'm sorry. I'll try to be better."

"I'm sure you will. Afterward all will be forgiven." He reached for her wrist and grasped it. "And hopefully a lesson will be learned."

"I've already learned my lesson. Believe me, I have."

He shook his head. "That won't work. It won't ever work with me."

He pulled her resisting figure over to a nearby stump. He sat and drew her over his lap.

"And I don't mean to frighten you, or hurt you capriciously. I only mean to teach you to obey."

He began to draw up the skirt of her gown, his hands skimming over the hem to touch her pale, lovely skin. His eyes drank in her shapely legs as they were revealed to him. She was rigid across his lap, blushing red.

"Everyone will see if you punish me here. Can't you do it somewhere more private?"

"No." If he took her anywhere private right now things would end only one way. "There's no one at work in the orchard this afternoon. If you are quiet enough, no one will know."

"Please!" she pleaded as he bared her bottom to his gaze, trying to cover herself with her hands. "Please, I'm—"

"Ashamed? You should be for your behavior today." He took her hands and held them fast at the small of her back. He couldn't help noticing how tiny they were. She was so delicate. Now, holding her petite frame across his lap, he was more certain than ever that she'd never withstand childbirth. All the more reason to rule her with a heavy hand. "Now lie still across my lap."

He spanked her once, watching the pink blush spread across her cheek. He spanked the other cheek and she moaned, a desperate pleading sound in her throat. He was only warming her up, just getting started. He intended to spank her soundly, but to his chagrin, he found himself distracted by her perfect, round globes. He spanked again, and again. She cried out and wiggled as a scarlet flush spread across her bottom. Spank marks soon rose to the surface. My God, the way she tensed waiting for the blows. The entire exercise was ridiculously arousing. *Focus.* The important thing was to teach her that disobedience was not acceptable. He increased the intensity, tightening his grip on her when she began to struggle.

"Please, that hurts! Please stop!"

"Hush."

He continued to rain strict, stinging spanks on her bottom until her fervent pleas turned to helpless moans and finally breathless sobs.

"Okay," he said finally, resting his hand on her trembling, bruised cheeks. "I believe I've made my point."

She didn't answer, only lay limp over his lap, her soft cries and whimpers a more erotic sound to him than any on earth.

"Okay," he murmured. "It's over now." He allowed himself one final caress, brushing his open palm slowly across her burning skin. He pulled her skirts back down over her lovely bottom, her silken thighs. He took a deep breath, trying to erase the memory before it drove him mad. He pulled her up into his lap. He held her as he'd promised to, cradling her close. She sobbed into his chest, squirming as her sore bottom contacted the hardness of his thighs.

Chapter Four

"Cait." He stroked her hair lightly. "It's over now. Do you feel you've learned your lesson?"

"Yes! I don't like it when you're angry with me. I don't ever want you to do that again. It hurt!"

"I hope it will hurt for a while, lass. I meant for it to. A lingering reminder." He rested his chin on top of her curls.

"But it...it feels good to be held," she whispered.

Lord, but the lass told the truth. It felt too good. His rod had begun to rise the moment he drew her skirt up. Now he was aching and heavy with need. He shifted, trying not to reveal the extent of his desire to her virginal eyes. He'd put her through enough for one afternoon.

"How long will you hold me?" she asked, nestling her head into his neck so that he felt the wetness of her tears.

Forever. As long as I possibly can. Which means I shouldn't be holding you at all.

"It's getting late, Caitlyn," he said. "We should return to the keep."

* * * * *

Cait slumped against his chest, enjoying the final moments of closeness with him. The rocking motion of the horse made her sore bottom smart anew with each step. Well, she had wanted his attention and she'd gotten it. Who knew when next she'd get it again? She was still considering if it had been worth it now that she'd had a taste of punishment over his lap. Devil indeed. It was an apt name for him, because her bottom hurt like the devil and his hand had given her pain like Beezlebub himself.

It had hurt more than anything she'd ever experienced. Perhaps she'd led a protected life in her cottage in the woods but she'd never, ever been struck in anger, with the intention to inflict pain. Even now her bottom throbbed, felt twice its usual size. But afterwards, to be cradled in his arms...that had made it all worthwhile.

She could have snuggled against him for an eternity. Never

mind that he had just spanked her so that she'd broken down in tears. It was all forgotten the moment he gathered her up in his arms and held her close. She had felt so lonely, so unwanted and bereft since Erma had died and circumstances had thrust her into the cold, wide world alone. It felt so amazing just to be held, just to be touched. Even if he'd only done it to get her down out of the tree, it was still the most wonderful moment she'd had in weeks.

Even now, leaning back against him while they returned to the courtyard, she still basked in his comforting warmth. How on earth had she not realized how cold she'd become? She shifted to press back even closer to him. Her thighs rested on top of his, and her head nestled perfectly under his chin so that each time he moved she could feel it. Closer, closer still…

"Enough." His voice rumbled against her ear. His hands clamped down on her hips, holding them away from him. "Sit still."

"It hurts."

"I know. It's supposed to. Now cease your squirming before everyone in town knows exactly what happened to you."

She blushed. Would they know? The townspeople threw many smiling glances their way. The earl and his new bride, how charming. Hopefully none of them realized what he'd just done to her. That would be too humiliating to bear. She looked down at his rough, suntanned hands on the reins in front of her. How striking they were. She'd known almost no men in her sheltered existence, and been this close to no other man at all, not ever in her life. She'd never even imagined a man might touch her where he'd touched her, on her bare skin, on her bottom, that he might hit her there so mercilessly with stinging, burning slaps. She supposed this type of thing must go on between man and wife or he wouldn't have done it so matter-of-factly to her.

But for her, there was nothing matter-of-fact about it. It had been a traumatic day, and she was awfully upset over what he'd forced her to submit to. Although to be honest, she had asked to be punished. She had intentionally disobeyed him and been quite disrespectful at the same time. He had told her exactly what would happen. She'd disobeyed him anyway and reaped the consequences.

So why did she feel more needful of him than ever? Why was she dismayed that they were almost to the keep?

He dismounted in the courtyard and lifted her down. His expression remained darkened by a frown.

"Are you still angry with me?" she asked.

"No. But I've wasted the better part of the afternoon dealing with your disobedience. I have work to do. I want you to go to your room and stay there until dinner and think over your behavior today."

"Yes sir."

"And Cait," he added, tilting her face up to his. "I expect to see you in the hall this evening sitting at my side, no matter how much the sitting hurts. Do not think for a minute of testing me and not being there."

"No sir."

He looked at her another long moment, and she wasn't sure what she read in his eyes. She still saw anger. She didn't know why. He said he was no longer angry with her, that afterward all would be forgiven. Perhaps he assumed she was terribly disobedient and expected her to disappoint him soon again. Well, she wouldn't. She would be the perfect wife. She would do whatever she had to do, whatever it took, if she could only get him to hold her like a treasure again.

* * * * *

It was absolutely intolerable what the girl did to his mind, not to mention the more sensual regions of his body. He pressed his cock in frustration. *Down, boy. Not now. Not ever.* He had no sympathy for her. He'd suffered at least as much as she had from the spanking, probably more.

He had work to do. He had to get his mind off her, but he'd see her at table. He decided that every day he would spend time with her at the evening meal. That would have to be enough. It would be safe; there would be nothing harmful he could do to her within sight of the entire hall. Time together with him would soothe her insecurities as a wife. He would give her his undivided attention, ask her about her day, gently touch her hand, share his cup with her. It would have to be enough. It was all he could safely give her. It would have to be enough for them both.

He thought for the millionth time that he ought to move her to a different bedroom. As it was, she was far too near. He fought the urge every night to stride through her door and drag her back to his bed. Or take her right there in her little maiden's bed. What difference did it make, as long as he was buried deep inside her? *No, no, no, no, no.*

There were other ways to be inside her. He would need to teach them to her soon or else risk going mad with lust for her, or risk getting her with child, which he wasn't going to do. Soon he would have to teach her, when the drive, when the desperate need wasn't so strong and he could be certain of staying in control.

Spanking her bare bottom hadn't helped matters. Even now he was replaying her punishment again in his mind. The lovely cries, the hapless kicking and squirming and struggling against him. The tensing of her supple, round, perfectly shaped buttocks—it was a miracle he hadn't come in his trousers from administering the punishment. And for some godforsaken reason, he'd walked the horse back to the grounds at slower than a snail's pace just to feel her fidget and shift in his arms. She was a sickness. Torture, plain and simple. She galled him and stole his reason and peace of mind.

He threw his energy into his duties and expended all his frustration on the practice fields where his men noticed a new edge to his fighting. He stayed longer than he should have, and found himself without much time to bathe before the dinner hour. To make matters worse, Henna came in to attend him, taking the opportunity to pour recriminations in his ear.

Chapter Four

"Duncan! What are you about now?" she lectured as she scrubbed his back. "She's upstairs crying on her bed looking as forlorn as a lost lamb!"

"What did she tell you?"

"She wouldn't say a thing, but I can see she's hurtin'. What did you do to the poor wee lass?"

"The poor wee lass disobeyed me directly and taunted me from the top of an apple tree. She got her bottom spanked for it."

Henna gasped in outrage.

"You didn't!"

"I did, and I will again if she won't stay safely by her guard. She knew the rule as well as the consequence, Henna, so keep your judgments to yourself."

"Well, I didn't raise you to be one of those who hurts a weaker creature than yourself, I really didn't! Especially a woman."

"Henna, I'm a soldier and an earl. I have to hurt 'weaker creatures' all the time. For what it's worth, I don't think much more was hurt than her pride and her sensibilities."

"For a woman, that kind of pain is the most humiliating and cruel."

"I have to disagree with you. It was important for me to show her who was in charge, and how important her safety is to me. I know it will surprise you to learn that I'm coming to care about the little scamp."

"Ha! If you cared about her you'd act differently. You refuse to make an honest wife of her and take her to your bed, and yet you're happy to turn her over your lap and punish her like an errant child when she makes one mistake. How do you think she feels, that you'll torment her defenseless bottom but haven't yet performed your husbandly duties as you should—"

"She feels nothing, because the ignorant chit has less than no idea what husbands and wives actually do. And I'd prefer it to stay that way as long as possible," he added with a stern look at Henna. "I'll introduce my wife to the intricacies of the marriage bed as soon as I see fit."

"Well," Henna harrumphed, scrubbing his back so hard he was sure she left marks, "I can't say I agree with the way you're treating her. Thought I raised you better, I did. Sometimes I think you're as cold as your father deep down inside."

"I am not like my father!" Duncan snapped. He bit his tongue hard to keep from saying words he'd regret, and stiffened under her hands. "Leave me now, Henna! I can abide no more of your squawking. Just leave me alone."

Wisely, in the face of Duncan's anger, the portly old woman made herself scarce.

Duncan sank back in the water with a frown. He was not his father's son. He never would be. No. His father was cold, emotionless, incapable of showing love or even empathy. Duncan was nothing like him, nothing at all. Was he? No, he wasn't, he couldn't be. He wouldn't be.

He rose up out of the tub and began to dry himself. It was time for dinner, time for him to sit and eat beside his wife. He needed to see her, desperately needed to be near her. Somehow her beauty, her innocent gaze, her crooked, uncertain smile would make it all okay.

Chapter Five

Duncan's hair was still wet when he arrived at the hall for dinner. His face hardened when he saw she wasn't there, but then he saw her approaching from the corridor. She turned her head a little, dropping her eyes from his. She was so charmingly shy. Or was she fearful? Ashamed perhaps? When she drew near he offered his hand and she took it, sliding him a look he didn't understand.

Well enough. Who understood women? Her duty now was to sit and eat beside him and as long as she did that, he didn't care what was going through her addled head. She sat on his left side, eating very little and speaking even less. She fidgeted plenty though, until he put a hand on her leg. She stilled, looking up at him.

I know. I meant for it to hurt.

"Aren't you hungry? You should eat. Your gowns are practically falling off you."

"These aren't my gowns."

He frowned. Why didn't his wife have any gowns of her own

yet? He'd have to ask Henna to remedy that quickly. She needed gowns that hugged every gorgeous curve. She should have a hundred beautiful gowns, all of them bright yellow, red, orange. Garish blazing colors so he could keep track of her when she ran off and climbed into trees. He chuckled under his breath.

"What is it?" she asked, pushing her food around her plate.

"Nothing." He watched her toy with her meal. It was obvious she was uncomfortable; not just uncomfortable sitting, but uncomfortable sitting next to him. It annoyed him, but he understood. "Put your fork down if you're finished eating."

"May I be excused?"

"No."

She placed her fork beside her plate and put her hands in her lap. Duncan swirled the wine in his glass, then offered her a sip.

"No thank you."

"Don't enjoy wine?"

"Not very much."

"Perhaps you've never had really fine wine."

"Perhaps I've had no wine at all," she said. "I'm just a nobody from a cottage in the woods."

He looked over at her sharply. "You aren't a nobody. You're my wife."

"I suppose."

I suppose. I suppose? What did she mean by that?

"There's no supposition about it." He narrowed his eyes. "You're my wife. The priest married us." She made no reply to that comment, only sat very still with her hands clasped in her lap.

"A cottage in the woods?" he asked, changing the subject. "You were not raised at court?"

She shook her head. No, of course not. If she had been, she wouldn't be such an innocent.

"My father hates me. No, I wasn't raised at court. He wouldn't have tolerated me there."

"He hates you? Why?"

"Because I remind him of my mother, and she was a liar and

Chapter Five

a slut."

He nearly spit out a mouthful of wine. "Who told you that? Your father? I'm sure it isn't true."

"I don't know. I never met my mother."

"Then who did you live with in your little cottage?"

"My nursemaid, Erma. She died a few weeks ago."

"And she didn't tell you anything about your mother? Or your father?"

She shook her head. "I never knew either of them."

"And you didn't ask? You weren't curious about your circumstances?"

"I didn't care. I didn't think about it. Erma was my family. I was happy there."

He frowned, not missing the insinuation. She *was* happy, but not anymore. "Can you not be happy here? I'll have some gowns made for you."

Gowns. *Idiot.* She was no typical, vain woman to be mollified with the promise of new gowns or pretty ribbons. He thought of the way she'd thrown the perfect apple down for him just a few hours earlier.

"I enjoy dining with you, Caitlyn. You're not a nobody to me."

"Thank you for saying that." She was obviously unconvinced. Then she asked again, "May I be excused?"

He sighed and nodded. "Yes."

* * * * *

Time passed, a couple of weeks, and Cait was pleased to be given many lovely gowns, but no more spankings over her husband's knee. It still occurred to her in lonelier moments to draw his attention through mischief, but the result was really too painful to make it worthwhile.

So she behaved as well as she could. She tolerated whichever surly young soldier followed her around, and did her best to stay out of the earl's way. She loved to be outside, strolling through the town watching the townspeople. She enjoyed watching the animals in the yards and the many children at play. The children avoided her for the most part, although she smiled at them. She supposed her strange appearance scared them away.

She found herself alone a lot, but it didn't matter. She was well cared for, content as she might be. She had plenty of fresh air and not many duties to attend to, although she begged for chores. She wanted to be put to work to escape her boredom, but Henna chased her from the kitchen and the laundry rooms whenever she lingered too long. The gardener at least let her help tend the gardens. The earl rolled his eyes when he discovered her dirty fingernails. He picked weeds from her curls, and told her she needn't till the soil like a common laborer. Thankfully, though, he didn't make her stop. If it wasn't for the solace of the garden, she would lose her mind.

The earl still ignored her as much as possible. He sat with her at dinner, yes, but they barely touched. They had trouble finding things to talk about since they knew each other so little. When he looked at her, which he did often, she always developed a lump in her throat that kept her from talking, from asking, from confiding, from saying any of the things she wanted to say.

How can I please you? What will make you like me? When will you hold me again?

She couldn't say them, so they went unanswered, and life went on as it was. And so it was that one day she was headed to the garden, hoping to catch a glimpse of the earl up on the rise when a strange man, tall and forbidding, stepped into her path.

She drew back. No man besides the earl dared come so near to her. She looked at her guard for guidance. He bowed to the man and said, "Good morning, my lord."

She looked back at the man warily. He looked very much like her husband, but he was older and his eyes were not nearly so kind. This man's eyes were hard and sharp, and they made her flush even though she'd no reason at all to feel ashamed.

Cait dropped a reserved curtsy. Her eyes went to the guard again, but he looked at the ground. It was Mitchum, the guard

Chapter Five

she'd gotten in so much trouble the first day. She'd apologized at least three times but he still looked on her with disdain. Now she felt glad to have him there, and sidled closer under the stranger's skewering gaze.

"Are you the earl's new wife? My daughter-in-law?"

"Yes. Yes sir," she replied.

"I am an earl too," he said with a sniff, "and your elder. It would be more courteous of you to refer to me as 'my lord.'"

Her eyes darted to his, and she felt indignant, but she only took a soft breath and curtsied again.

"Like most women, I suppose you rely on your charms rather than your manners to bring those around you to heel."

She raised her chin a bit. "I don't bring anyone to heel, sir. My lord," she remembered with a small frown.

He laughed, and his laughter didn't have a mirthful sound. "I'll believe it when I see it." He looked at Mitchum, sizing him up. "Run along, boy. I'll talk to my new daughter-in-law alone."

Cait's eyes flew to Mitchum's in alarm. He looked back at her with an unfathomable look and stood up a little straighter. "I'm not to leave my lady. Direct orders from my lord, the earl. For her protection," he added with a hint of pride.

"Protection? And what harm will come to her in my company, in full view of the keep and the townspeople below?"

Mitchum seemed to consider. It would be most impolite for him to contradict the older man's order, but Cait didn't want him to leave her alone. He looked at Cait briefly.

"I beg your pardon, my lord, but I serve the earl."

She spoke up in his defense. "I'm not permitted to be without a guard no matter what. Or my husband punishes me," she added, coloring a bit.

"Oh, does he?" That seemed to amuse the earl greatly. "And how does my son punish his wayward wife?"

Cait bowed her head. "I...I cannot say. I would rather not."

The earl laughed long and loud then.

"You will not say. I see. Aren't you a sassy bit of a wife?"

"No sir. My lord."

"But I say you are. I can see you are a most insubordinate type. Never mind. Where is my son? I'll go and find him. I can offer plenty of advice on how to subdue a willful wife. I've had enough of them," he added archly, before turning on his heel and dismissing them both with his broad back.

She stood there, shocked to stillness by his rude behavior. She turned to Mitchum, who looked back at her in silent accord.

"What an unpleasant man," she said. "Thank you, Mitchum, for not leaving." She started towards the garden, her mind troubled. "I don't think I'd care to be with him alone."

"I need no thanks. The earl charges me to stay by you, lady, and so I do."

"You can call me Caitlyn if you like. My friends call me Cait."

"I canna call you Cait or Caitlyn, lady. But I appreciate the offer all the same. And I think..." His voice trailed off uncertainly. "I think you would do best, lady, not ever to be alone with the older earl."

She stopped again, looking at him soberly.

"Thank you, Mitchum, for your sage advice. I'll be sure to let the earl know how faithfully you serve him."

"Yes, ma'am," replied Mitchum with a shadow of a smile.

* * * * *

That night at dinner Cait was relieved that the older man, Lord Douglas, was seated on the opposite side of her husband. She still heard his jibes to his son about his saucy wife. If she had her wish she wouldn't have come to the table at all while he was there. She would rather have stayed to her room until he was gone. She couldn't explain it, but Lord Douglas caused her a deep uneasiness. Even her father had not frightened her so much. And though she didn't look at him, had no intention of ever meeting his cold hard eyes again, she felt them on her and it made something shivery and sick coil in her belly. Surely it would anger the earl if she showed disrespect to his father, but

Chapter Five

she didn't think she could smile at him no matter how hard she tried.

Fortunately her husband seemed to sense her discomfort. He sent her to her room the minute she'd finished her meal. Perhaps he only tired of listening to his father's disparaging banter about her. Either way, it was with relief that she stood to exit the hall.

"Wait!" his father said. "Is that how you take leave of your husband's table?"

Cait froze, and her eyes flew to her husband's.

"It is no matter," Duncan said. "We don't keep formal manners here."

"We do at my keep, and I'm accustomed to the ladies taking their leave with a pleasant curtsy and a 'good eve.'"

Her husband looked at her, the color rising around his neckline, whether from anger or embarrassment, she didn't know. She dipped into a half-hearted curtsy and managed, through great effort, to meet the awful man's eyes.

"Good eve to you, my lord."

"And good eve to you, lass," he replied in a voice dripping with disdain.

Cait felt absolutely humiliated.

"Good eve, Caitlyn," said Duncan quietly, although she heard the fury in his tone.

She fled to the shelter of her room and shut the door. It was a warm night but she shivered violently. She climbed into bed, pulling the covers over her head. But she couldn't get warm and she couldn't rest even when the keep quieted around her. She felt a strange agitation that wouldn't let her sleep. When she closed her eyes, Lord Douglas's visage rose before her, and she feared if she fell asleep he would come to her in her dreams.

At last, she crept from her bed and over to the door, the door to the room she'd been warned, on pain of punishment, never to enter. His room. She didn't know if he'd yet retired for the night, but she was too unquiet to stay in her room alone.

She turned the heavy lock, the lock Henna checked every night. It opened with a soft click. She pushed the door and peeked into the moonlit darkness.

He was there, staring right at her from the bed.

* * * * *

Duncan was still awake, fuming over his father's unannounced visit. Pretty much every word he'd spoken since he arrived had been some form of criticism or disrespect. And his father's treatment of Caitlyn... It had taken every measure of his hard-won control and self-discipline to keep from throttling the old man to death by the neck.

His rudeness to her at dinner had been insupportable. She had looked to Duncan to save her, and he ought to have defended her, but it only would have fed his father's ire and prolonged a humiliating episode he was certain his father enjoyed. Instead, all he'd wanted to do was get her away from his father's presence. His father loved to insult and embarrass women, but it was something else altogether to see it visited on Cait. Until Douglas left, he'd do a better job of protecting her. He'd be sure to tell her guards to do the same.

He wondered if she was angry with him for not defending her, and whether she had cried after she scurried from the hall. Well, of course she'd cried. She cried at everything. He had the sudden urge to check on her, just to peek into her room and be sure she was sleeping. It couldn't hurt, could it? The door would be locked, but he could use the hall door. And if she was still awake, he could hold her, soothe her. Explain that it wasn't her fault, that it was his father, that he was the one flawed...

But no, if he held her there would be no explaining. There would be no talking or soothing or anything except him ripping off her shift and burying himself to the hilt between her thighs.

With a soft groan, he felt his member pulse to life just imagining it. Just imagining it for a second was enough to keep him up all night. He was just about to take himself in hand when he heard the lock click, a tiny sound, but unmistakable. The door opened a crack, and her haunting eyes peered through the half light of the moon to meet his. She gasped softly, but she didn't close the door. Instead, she opened it wider and sidled into his room, pressing back against the door as if, that way, she might not break the rule about entering.

He watched her from where he sat, in a conundrum. He was unclothed and fully aroused. There was no way to rise from the bedclothes and show himself to her without frightening her right back out of the room. And he didn't want her to leave, because she was obviously troubled. The very fact that she would break his emphatic rule and enter his room was evidence of that.

So he sat right where he was and waited to hear her speak.

"I...I'm sorry to disobey you. I...I had to come in." The poor thing was terrified he'd be angry. It touched him, how upset she was to be breaking his rule.

"Why did you have to come in?" he prompted softly.

"B...Because...I'm cold."

He frowned. "It's not at all cold, Caitlyn. It's warm tonight, so if you're cold, I'm afraid you may be ill. Come here to the bed. Let me check for fever."

She pulled her blanket more tightly around her shoulders. Nice try. He could have it off her in an instant, and the flimsy shift she wore beneath. She approached him as if she knew there were danger. He reached out to place roughened fingers against her forehead, then down the side of her face, against her porcelain cheeks. He looked into her eyes.

"No fever. You feel fine to me. Are you really cold, or do you have another reason for being here? Do not tell lies, Caitlyn. I don't like it."

"I...I..."

"Were you upset by my father today?"

"Yes," she whispered in relief. "He...scares me a little."

"I completely understand. He dealt with you very rudely and I apologize for it, although I'm sure he'll do it again. You must understand that's just his way. Unfortunately, he is my father, so you must show him respect as far as you can."

"Yes sir." He knew she would, only because he asked it of

her. She really was remarkably obedient. His cock throbbed from the trusting, open way she looked at him. She leaned closer so he could feel her heat. The sweetness of her soft breath washed over him, stealing his control.

"I'm...I'm so sorry if I embarrassed you. If you were displeased with me..."

"I was not displeased. I am never displeased with you. I know I..." Without meaning to, he reached to take a lock of her black hair between his fingers, twirling it. "I know it seems I am distant, that I don't care for you. But Caitlyn, there's a reason for that."

Silence stretched out between them.

"What reason?" she finally asked.

Duncan frowned. "I'm not really certain if you're ready yet to become my true wife."

She drew a soft breath of surprise. "What...what do you mean? Your true wife?"

He dropped her hair and ran his knuckles down her velvet cheek.

"Wives and husbands, they can share certain...intimacies with each other if they wish. But it requires bravery, and hard work."

"What kind of work?" she asked, so eagerly that it touched his heart. "I'm good at doing work. I don't mind it at all."

"I know, Caitlyn. But it's hard, complicated work, like no work you've done before. And it takes a lot of practice and a lot of courage. I'm not sure you're ready for it."

"No," she protested, wide-eyed. "I am. If you'll just teach me, I promise I will do whatever you wish."

If you'll just teach me... If she hadn't said those words to him, he might have been able to resist. If she hadn't said them so beautifully, with that perfect balance of eagerness and submission, he might have found the strength to say, *no, not yet. You're still too innocent to be used the way I want to use you.* But she had said the words perfectly, and then, as if that wasn't enough to break him, she'd followed with *I promise I will do whatever you wish.*

Chapter Five

What could he do? Such words were impossible to withstand.

So he put his hands on the coarse wool blanket she'd wrapped around herself and said, "All right. I'll teach you, Caitlyn. If you're absolutely sure you're ready to learn."

Chapter Six

He took the blanket from around her shoulders and laid it across his bed, so she stood before him clothed only in her shift. It was thin, fine linen and it left nothing to his imagination, but she seemed to believe it offered her some protection, because when he reached for the ties of it, she frowned.

"You are not ready," he said.

"No, I am. But will I...will you...?"

"In this room, Caitlyn, when we are alone together, you will be unclothed. As soon as you enter this room you'll bare yourself for me immediately, every time. Do you know why that is?"

"No," she whispered, blushing furiously, but letting his fingers untie the ivory ribbons one by one.

"Because in this room, your body will belong to me. Your husband. And I will enjoy looking at it whenever and however I please."

"Oh," she said as he drew the flimsy garment away from her. By pure instinct, her hands sought to cover her breasts, her mons.

"And you will not hide yourself from me, of course. Wives do not do that. Not obedient wives, anyway."

Slowly, her hands dropped to her sides.

"Let me look at you. You are a beautiful woman."

"Am I?"

But he didn't answer. He couldn't find the words. His hands basked on her skin, ran over the curve of her waist, the taut flatness of her belly, the hard tips of her aroused nipples. He ran his thumb over the dusky pink peaks and almost lost himself when she gasped and closed her eyes. Without thinking, he leaned over to take her in his mouth. First one lovely breast and then the other, laving and nibbling the treasures with his tongue and lips.

She moaned, her fingers scrabbling on his shoulders.

"Oh, this isn't work. This isn't hard at all!"

He chuckled, releasing her.

"There's more to it than that, lovely girl. Go kneel by the window, in the moonlight, so I can take a long look at you." She obeyed, looking over at him with breathless, aroused confusion.

"Like this?" she asked. *Yes, like that. Submissive and open and sweet.*

"Yes, very good. Keep your back straight and your chin up, and look at me. I'll expect you to look at me when we're...doing what husbands and wives do, so you'll know what I want of you at all times."

At that, he finally threw the bedclothes off and stood, walking towards her with his cock fisted in his hand. He could see she lost her nerve a little then, although she tried bravely not to show it. It wouldn't surprise him at all if this was her first introduction to the aroused male anatomy.

He stood before her in the moonlight, taking her chin in his hands.

"This is the hard part, and it may seem unnatural, but I want you to kiss me. There," he said, indicating the part of his body she surely couldn't miss.

"Yes...yes sir."

"Do you know how to kiss, Caitlyn? Have you ever been

kissed by a man before?"

"No. Not actually."

"Stand up." He pulled her up by her arms. He kissed her at length, gently at first, then more deeply. She shuddered and sighed, pressing against him. God, she was making this difficult with her gorgeous, innocent reactions. He wrapped his arms around her slender waist and pulled her close. His hands strayed lower to cup her heart-shaped bottom in his hands. He finally broke from her, afraid of losing control.

"Okay. That's how you kiss, Caitlyn, and you remember how tenderly I kissed you there," he reminded, tugging gently on her puckered nipples.

"Yes, I remember."

"Back to your knees then. Take me in your hands. God, yes... like that." It would be a miracle if he lasted until she put her lips on him. Just the feel of her trembling fingertips caressing him was enough to make a drop of pre-cum shimmer on the head of his cock. "Now lick it. Kiss it. Just the tip."

She rose up on her knees to position her mouth before him, and her pink tongue darted out to taste him. She licked him artlessly, clumsily, but he screwed his eyes shut and tensed to keep himself from shooting all over her face.

"Yes. Yes, that's good," he said through clenched teeth.

"Am I hurting you?"

"No. Don't stop. Now open your mouth wide, and take me between your lips. Let me slide into your mouth."

Miracle of miracles, she opened for him. This had been the point where Lenore balked, where she'd turned on him and called him unnatural. A depraved, perverse villain. And he was all those things, but bless Cait, she didn't know.

He thrust in her then, as deeply as he dared without alarming her, cupping her face gently to guide his cock in and out. He was going to come, and he was going to come hugely.

"Cait," he gasped. "Very soon I'm going to release in your mouth. It's going to taste strange and viscous, but you're not to spit it out. You're to swallow it. It won't hurt you. Do you

Chapter Six

understand?"

She nodded, and he grasped the back of her neck, groaning long and hard as he discharged in her throat. He felt her choke a little, but she swallowed him as best she could. Astonishing. Not one cry of displeasure or outrage. He pulled her up, overcome by the intimacy of the moment. He enveloped her in his arms and kissed her.

"Good girl. I know it wasn't easy."

She nuzzled against him, trembling in his grasp.

"Did I please you? I tried my best."

"You did very well for the first time. Very well. And it will get easier in time. With practice."

"How...how often...?" She wasn't quite able to say the words.

"Every day, at least for a little while, until it becomes more natural to you," he said, stroking her hair. "It pleases me very much to be inside you, to feel your warm mouth around me, pleasuring me. I'll want you to do it quite often." He chuckled at her expression. "I told you it would be work. But I promise there will be pleasure for you too."

"There will?"

"Yes. If you obey me. Go to the bed, Cait. Lie down on your back. Trust me," he said when she hesitated.

Drawing a deep breath, she turned from him and walked to the bed. She lay back, looking at him with wide eyes. He felt his cock tighten again. Just a look from her fathomless eyes could undo him. The image of her taking his cock in her mouth would stay with him forever. He would be hard for a week just remembering it.

"Spread your legs. Open them," he said. She did, just a little, the modesty ingrained in all women hampering her. "Wider. I want to see you there. Wider," he urged her repeatedly, until her thighs were spread wide apart and he could see the luscious treasure between her legs. He stood and admired her for a long moment. His cock was already hard again, but he wouldn't take her that way. He knelt instead, pulling her to the edge of the bed and spreading her legs. He could tell she felt exposed. Her legs tensed and she tried to close them, but he pinned her open. He dipped his mouth to her, blowing hot breath on her beautiful pink pussy. She squirmed. His hands tightened on her thighs.

"Be still. Let me have you. Be a good girl for me."

And she was, oh, she was. He began to kiss her, lick her, lightly at first. She was so exquisite, so erotically sensitive, even the softest tease of his tongue made her buck under him. She tasted beautiful, musky and female.

"Oh, oh..." Her soft cries drove him on, and the way she moved, the way she writhed and sighed—he could have eaten her alive.

"Yes. Let yourself go for me."

She moaned as he licked and caressed her. She was searching for something, and he knew she hadn't the slightest idea what. He would help her find it. He would help her learn the depths of pleasure she was capable of experiencing, no matter how long it took.

He soothed her, then urged her on with his mouth until she was breathless and tense with coiled desire.

"Let go." He breathed against her. "I've got you."

She was gasping quick, heady gasps. Her hands twisted and twined in his hair. Carefully, he slid one finger up inside her slick opening, and both of them moaned. Jesus, she was so tight, so impossibly hot and slick. It was some kind of madness, that he didn't stand up and thrust inside. He regained control of himself, concentrating on her pleasure. He bit and nipped gently at her clit, that little nub hard and swollen under his mouth. He thrust a second finger inside her and she gasped at the fullness, threw her head back and wailed. He felt her come, her velvet walls pulsing and clenching against his fingers. He didn't remove them until she'd relaxed again, until her breathing slowed. She lay completely still, as if she understood the peril she was in, although she didn't. Of that he was sure. He looked down at her, longing, craving. He touched her cheek lightly, tried to smile. Tried to reassure her in the face of the words he had to say.

"Caitlyn. I think it's better if you don't stay here. If you go back to your room to sleep."

"Oh." The disappointment on her face, the forlorn way her eyebrows drew together... "Wh...Why? I'm sorry..."

"No, it's nothing you did. It's me, Caitlyn. I'll tire you out. I'll want your mouth again and again and it's not fair to you. You must go and rest now. It's late."

"I'll do anything, please, if you'll just let me stay. Whatever you want! I don't want to leave. Please hold me in the dark while I sleep. I'm afraid to be alone."

He stood over her, looking down at her. If he let her stay now, she'd expect to stay every night.

"Am I not your true wife now? I tried my best. I'll keep practicing, I will—"

"Enough, Caitlyn." She killed him. It was true, she had done everything he'd asked of her, been a more true and obedient wife than Lenore had ever been. It was the tears shimmering in her eyes that finally undid him.

"Okay." He frowned. It was a terrible idea, and it increased the danger to her significantly, but there was no way now to say no.

"I'll be quiet," she promised. "I won't disturb you. I'll lie very still."

No matter, he thought. It had nothing to do with that. She could lie still as the grave, be quiet as a mouse in a cat's sight, and he'd still burn to make her his. Now that he'd felt her, thrust his fingers up inside her hot, tight channel, he didn't know how he would resist. Perhaps if he exhausted himself each day in exertions, he could fall fast asleep at night with her beside him in his arms.

Folly, to think there was anyway he could manage to leave her alone.

"Kneel down, then, Cait," he said, showing her his engorged cock. "Once more, so we can get to bed."

* * * * *

Douglas waited until the castle was quiet. He could lurk about wherever he wanted, he was the elder earl after all. No one would tell him what to do. But he didn't want to lurk about just anywhere. He'd planned all day, since the moment he saw her, to pay a very furtive and quiet visit to his pretty little daughter-in-law in the night.

All in the family, yes? She was his son's wife, and if she could take Duncan's coarse cock between her legs, she could spread her thighs nice and wide for his. He'd clamp his hand over her mouth so she couldn't scream and bring everyone running. It would be made all the more thrilling to know his son slept right next door, unaware.

Yes, he'd figured out all the particulars as soon as he decided he wanted her. Located her bedroom, insured that his son would be asleep before he went to her. It was all made much easier by the fact that Duncan elected to sleep apart from her.

Well, he didn't blame him. Once the wife had been fucked, had yielded what was between her legs, what else was she good for? Keeping you awake? Driving you insane with mindless women's prattle? Snuggling up against you, trying to steal your warmth? A saucy bit of goods like Duncan's wife was good for one thing and one thing only, and Douglas intended to go and take it from her by force.

She wouldn't give it up to him voluntarily, he was sure of that. If she would have, it wouldn't have to get as ugly as it was going to be. She would fight and he would have to subdue her. Well, that was most of the fun, wasn't it? It would give him a delicious thrill to see her eyes wild with fear as he choked off her breath. He would make it known without words that she would have to comply, or else. Luckily, women were so easy to overpower, especially for a man of his strength.

And if she dared try to tell Duncan what he was up to, he would smooth things over and let the little slut know exactly what happened to girls who told. He sighed, stroking himself. His cock twitched at the thought of disciplining the little bitch. That's what he really wanted to do, hurt the disrespectful little cunt. The way she looked at him sideways with those impertinent eyes. The contemptuous curl to her lips when she refused to smile at him. Oh, he'd like an hour or two alone with her, with some rope, a gag, and a whip.

He'd fix it so she never looked a man in the eyes again, much less with that insolent cast to her gaze. The pretty thing must lead his spineless son around by the cock to not know better, to act so disrespectfully to him in front of all his townspeople. One day he'd find a way to mete out discipline to her, since his son didn't have the nerve.

For now he'd have to content himself with what he could most easily take, for what he could give her with his hand clamped over her mouth. After he used her front, he thought he might flip her over and use her backside. That would teach her a thing or two about acting disrespectfully towards a man.

His cock was throbbing now with need. He looked up and down the upper corridor and found himself alone. He crept to her door and slid it open. He eased inside, letting his eyes adjust to the darkness. In the moonlight, he saw her bed was empty. *Damn.* His eyes flew around the small room, but she definitely wasn't there. He would sit on her bed and wait a few moments for her to return. But she would scream if she saw him. It would be better to wait for her behind the door. He could cover her nose and mouth at the same time until she ceased to struggle, until she didn't have breath to scream.

He stroked his cock, imagining the feeling of her small body struggling against him. He stroked it a long while. Too long a while. When a good many minutes had passed he realized she wasn't returning at all.

Little slut, where was she? A midnight rendezvous with a lover? Fucking whore. Or had she decided, this night of all nights, to stay in Duncan's bed?

Well, eventually he would get her, he'd find a way. He'd get to her one way or another, and she would be so, so sorry when he did.

Cait and the Devil

*****

Duncan knew he should have slept, but instead he lay awake gazing down at her. It wasn't as difficult to bide near her in the night time as he'd thought. It was hard when she had been awake, yes, and available to him. But now, in sleep, she looked far too angelic and sweet to molest.

He looked at her without agitation and need, now that he was controlled, relaxed...satisfied. He'd taken her mouth again before she crawled into his arms, snuggled into his chest as if she wished to merge with him completely. Her small bones had poked into him, but he hadn't had the heart to nudge her away. She had so selflessly given him pleasure, and accepted his seed once again in her mouth and her throat without a word of complaint.

Now those luscious lips were curved in a faint smile. She breathed steadily in and out. Every so often her eyelashes fluttered as if she was dreaming. Her fingertips would tighten against his hard muscles and she would shift even closer again.

No, it was not so difficult to resist her in the night. Not so difficult while she was sleeping like a hapless kitten in the shelter of his arms. He wondered what it was that made her so averse to being alone. Whatever it was, it had started something between them, and relieved the ache in his cock. Soon he would begin to train her to take him in the other way, in the other passage a woman had that didn't lead to a child. The idea of plumbing that tight, forbidden channel excited him, but he would be sure to prepare her first so she would be ready for him.

He had so many things to teach her now, now that he knew she was willing. He would teach her all she needed to know to be his submissive, attentive wife. In return, he would train her to feel unbelievable heights of pleasure without any inhibition or shame. He smiled down at her innocent face in sleep. *Just you wait.*

He had no doubt he could take her to those places. She seemed not to have the natural reticence and discomfort with her body that most women had. Perhaps being raised in seclusion with an old woman had its advantages. If no one ever taught you to feel shame, you didn't know what it was. You didn't know when your wedded husband was visiting it upon you, or if you did, you enjoyed it so much you didn't care.

Yes, he was already thinking about the daring things he was going to do to her. He was certain she would be an apt and willing pupil as long as he treated her with care. Of course, he would still punish her sometimes when she needed it. Or when he wanted it, whichever happened first. He'd have to really put his mind to finding reasons to punish her. The lass had an obedient streak a mile wide.

* * *

Cait awoke with a start in the dark hours of the morning. She turned and reached for him. Yes, he was still there. She cuddled close to him, as close as she dared without waking him. His rough chest, his soothing heat relaxed her. It seemed she'd wanted this forever, to be cradled in his arms. To feel appreciated, valued, wanted. The way he'd gazed at her after she'd pleased him with her mouth made her thrill with happiness and pride.

But as she slept she had a terrible dream of the old earl, Lord Douglas, and then a haunting vision of a lady in woad blue who'd urged her to protect herself. Protect herself from what? From Lord Douglas? She knew well enough that she needed protection from him. She had no intention of ever being caught by him alone. But it seemed the woman who'd berated her to protect herself had been talking about more than Duncan's father.

And the woman had looked exactly like Cait herself.

She had looked like an older version of Cait, only taller and more willowy, and much more vehement in her manner and tone. What did it mean? The entire dream alarmed her. She pressed her forehead to Duncan's chest and breathed in his clean, masculine scent. Duncan would protect her. He'd never told her as much in words, but she knew it, had known it with a strange certainty from her earliest moments with him. Even when he'd pushed her away, even the time he'd punished her, she'd known he cared for her well-being, in no small part because of his insistence on her having a guard.

Now, she would stay shoulder to shoulder with her guard until Lord Douglas was gone. Even then, she would forever more be careful.

Protect yourself! the woman had implored.

Who was the woman? Would Duncan be enough to protect her? With that fretful thought, she drifted off to sleep again, too tired now to dream. She woke to the strong light of late morning, disappointed to find herself alone. But of course, he had many important duties to attend to.

She stretched, feeling warm and content, when a soft knock sounded and Henna bustled in. Her smile was so wide that Cait giggled in spite of herself.

"Oh, I see you there, you saucy lass. Did you have a good night, did you, then? I see you did."

Cait couldn't wipe the proud smile from her face. "Yes. Now I'm a true wife to the earl!"

"I bet you are," laughed Henna. "And it's high time. I told you he would be a good husband to you. And did you enjoy becoming a true wife to him?"

"Yes. It was a quite bit of work, but...there were good parts too."

"Quite a bit of work?" Henna crowed in amusement. "Oh, you little sauce. And so now, perhaps, you'll soon be a mother."

Cait's brows drew together in confusion.

"Oh...? Yes, perhaps."

Henna rolled her eyes.

"Ya know nothing at all about it, do ya, lass? Well, when your husband plants his seed inside you, that's how a baby grows. He did plant his seed inside you, didn't he?" she added suspiciously.

Chapter Six

Cait blushed, thinking back to the thick, warm liquid she'd swallowed.

"Yes, he planted his seed in me twice, actually. And then..." Her mind worked over things. "A baby grows in your stomach?"

She thought of the pregnant women she'd seen, their waists swollen large. It all suddenly made sense.

"Yes, that's exactly how it happens, more or less." Henna nodded. "Someday we'll talk about it more. When your own belly starts to grow. Soon enough now I'm sure, now that you're made a true wife."

"Yes, I think a baby will grow very soon, Henna. He said..." She blushed, remembering his words. "He's going to plant seeds in me every day. So it shouldn't take long."

"Every day!" exclaimed Henna with an indulgent smile. "Well, then! Very good of him, surely. An excellent plan."

Chapter Seven

A child, thought Cait as she sat at dinner. Incredible. She might already be growing a child. The idea of it was so surprising, so delightful, even Lord Douglas's glowering couldn't dampen her mood. She loved children. She would love to have one of her own, one that wouldn't run away from her like the town children did. No, she would be her darling child's mama. She would never, ever let her child come to harm or feel unwanted or unloved. Best of all, her child would have Duncan for a father. Her child would be half-Duncan, half-Cait.

The idea of it was just so wonderful. She couldn't wait to return to his room tonight and talk to him about it. She wondered why he hadn't mentioned it the night before, told her the reason for the intimate activities they'd done. She would have done anything to please him, but knowing it was to make a baby would have made her that much more eager to do as he asked. She didn't understand how the things he'd done to *her* fit into the puzzle, but she liked them way too much to ask questions that might cause him to stop.

Chapter Seven

Maybe it was better if she didn't mention anything about a baby either. She remembered his first wife had died in childbirth. Perhaps the idea of babies and children reminded him of her, and that's why he'd said nothing about it. She didn't want to make him sad or bring up painful memories. She decided she shouldn't mention babies at all, not until he brought it up, or until her belly grew so large it would have to be discussed.

She wondered how long it took to grow a baby. She would have to have a long talk with Henna soon.

"Eat, Caitlyn." Duncan pointed at the food on the plate she'd barely touched. "You'll need your strength for later," he said under his breath.

She shivered and got goosebumps all over.

"Yes sir."

She began to eat with a better appetite. After all, it probably took lots of good, healthy food for a baby to grow.

* * * * *

Duncan looked over at his wife. He'd missed her terribly all day, and was looking forward to retiring to his bedroom with her as soon as their meal was done.

Improving his mood even more was news that a disruption in his father's lands called him away. He would be leaving early in the morning. Not a moment too soon. Lord Douglas had tired of haranguing him about his wife, choosing instead this evening to grouse over his meal, criticizing the cooks, the servants, and the "worthless wenches" who kept his cup filled.

He was an unhappy, bitter old man who had made his childhood a living hell. Good riddance to the devil. He hoped he didn't return anytime soon. He knew Cait would be pleased to hear he was leaving.

Cait.

He needed her soon.

"Are you finished?" he asked with a soft edge of urgency.

"You just told me to eat."

"Yes, eat, quickly. Eat." He leaned back, schooling his desire to patience. While he waited he would think about what to teach her tonight, what pleasures to visit on her beautiful body. No, that perhaps wasn't the best idea, he thought, shifting to accommodate the sudden fullness in his trousers.

"Are you done yet?" he asked for the second time in a minute.

Cait slid a sideways look at him. "Yes, I guess I am."

Duncan took her by the elbow and lifted her from her chair.

"Bid my father goodnight." He barely gave her time to drop a curtsy before he dragged her toward the door. She tripped along as gracefully as she could, trying for all the world to appear as if he wasn't pulling her off to bed.

At the door to his room he looked down at her.

"Will you spend the night again, Cait?"

"Yes." She nodded shyly, squeezing his hand. He opened the door and ushered her inside.

"Do you remember what I taught you?"

She nodded and began to remove her gown, her stockings, her underthings until she stood before him unclothed, the moonlight shining on her lovely skin.

"And why do you undress for me when we're in this room, Cait?" he prompted in a low voice.

"Because my body belongs to you, and you can look at it whenever you like."

"Yes, Caitlyn, in the privacy of this bedroom. I don't want you ever showing it to anybody else."

"No, my lord. Never."

"My name is Duncan." He ran his fingers over her shoulders and down to the tips of her breasts. "Why do you never call me that?"

"I don't know," she said, then gasped when he pinched her nipples. She leaned close to him, wanting him to hold her. He took her in his arms and kissed her, then whispered against her lips.

"Do you like it when I touch you that way, Caitlyn?"

"Whenever you touch me, I like it," she said, pressing closer to him.

"Undress me, wife."

Caitlyn began to remove his clothes, but she did it so gingerly that he ended up doing most of it himself. She laid his clothes over the chest beside the bed, and he let her, so he could watch her move across the room and back. His cock was twitching to be inside her. *Patience, Duncan. Not too fast.*

"Come here," he said. "Come sit here and tell me what you did today."

She sat beside him on the bed and began to relate her day's activities. As she did, he laid her back and spread her legs, stroking her there, finding her wet and ready for him. *No, not there. Not like that.* He knelt, and her voice cut off abruptly.

"Keep talking, Cait. You met Henna in the kitchen..."

"Yes, I met Henna in the kitchen because she had promised to show me how to dry and press flowers..." Her voice trailed off as she arched her hips against him and moaned.

"How to dry and press flowers..." he prompted her.

"Yes...yes...and then...then I went to the garden. I looked for roses. Gordon said I could...oh..."

She made a pleading noise and his hands tightened on her thighs. "Go on."

"And then...then...I returned to the hall to luncheon, which I ate outside the kitchen with Jeremy...and then...oh, Duncan—" she groaned, bucking under his mouth. "Please!"

With a sigh against her lovely folds, he delved one single finger up inside her slick passage, then another, while he pressed a third slick finger to the other, tighter opening and pressed gently against it. She tensed, but he was slow and gentle.

"Relax. I'm trying to make you feel good. Does that feel good, Caitlyn?"

"Duncan...oh...please...God..."

"Does it feel good?" he repeated, moving his fingers slowly against her. "Tell me the truth, Cait. Never lie to me."

"Yes. Yes, it feels good."

"And what did you do after lunch, Caitlyn?"

"After lunch? Oh, I...I took a walk in town and stopped to talk to the milliner...oh..."

Again he put his mouth, his lips, his tongue on her, but his fingers never stopped their wicked teasing and probing. He could feel her growing tense.

"And then?" he asked, nipping at her clit. "What did you talk about with the milliner?"

"I don't...I can't...I don't remember...I can't think of it now."

"Would you like to come?"

"What?" She was writhing under him, straining for release. "What...what does that mean?"

"I'll show you." He licked her, caressing her slick petals with sure strokes of his tongue. At the same time, he thrust his fingers deep inside her, as deeply as he could. She gasped, and then she fell apart.

"Oh, Duncan!" she cried out, arching up to him, shaking with wonder and pleasure.

"Yes, Cait, I know." His fingers and mouth didn't stop until her orgasm passed and she lay back, limp and satiated. He stroked her black curls, mussed and wild now.

"Rest a little bit," he said, "and then it will be your turn to please me." He stood, stroking his cock, and waited to see if she would balk. But no, she looked at him with...God...admiration. Her face softened into a kind of hopefulness. *She wanted him.* It took his breath away.

How many times had Lenore looked on him with hatred, with disgust and revulsion as he approached her? Even the women he'd bedded with coin or because they took pity on him, they'd never looked at him like this. He leaned over her and kissed her, burying his fists in her hair, savoring the taste of her lips. Finally, he broke away from her.

"I desire you so much," he whispered against her lips.

"You do?"

"Yes. I'll show you how much."

He pulled her up from the bed and without being asked she fell to her knees and waited as he guided his cock to her lips.

Chapter Seven

"Open up, yes. You remember. Just like that."

He thought it would be easier to find control the second night, but the sight of her lips gripping his cock was as erotic as ever. He gritted his teeth, trying to hold back as long as possible. The slick warmth of her mouth, her willing ministrations sent a pulse pounding through his veins to his balls, his thighs. He thrust deeper inside her throat, making her gag.

"It's okay," he said when she tensed. "It takes practice. I know. Try your best. Use your hands, don't be afraid. Caress me while you do it, just as I caressed you."

Her timid fingers explored him, but most of her attention centered on his cock and dealing with its repeated invasion of her mouth. Soon he could feel his crisis approaching, a rising wave, a tightening . As a signal he threaded his fingers in the back of her hair.

"Don't pull away. I'm going to come in your throat."

She moaned and was still, accepting his offering without distaste when it came.

"Good girl," he sighed, pulling away from her. "Now, stay right where you are. I want to look at you."

She was so beautiful, her mouth relaxed and glistening, her back straight, her pale eyes looking up at him from beneath black lashes. He knelt down beside her and kissed her. He caressed her hips, her bottom, her breasts, enjoying the velvety soft womanliness of her, and then he cupped her face in his hands.

"I'm going to do some things to you now, my love. You need only to obey. Do you understand?"

"Will...Will you hurt me?"

"I might. A little. Just a little bit."

"Why?" Her gaze was troubled. "Are you angry with me?"

"No, I'm not angry at all. I just want you so very badly. I want to show you some things I enjoy, but they may feel strange and frightening at first. They may hurt a little. What I want you to do is endure these things anyway. Endure them for me."

"Okay," she said, not fully understanding. He could tell she was frightened, yet she still wanted to please him. He wanted to reassure her, but she needed to learn on her own how to cope with the demands he would make.

"Do you love me, Duncan?" she asked suddenly with wide eyes, as if she read his very thoughts. "You just called me your love."

"Yes, I love you, little Cait. Never more than at times like this. Now listen to me, and obey me."

"Yes, my lord. I'll try."

He ran his fingertips down her back, thinking of the least frightening way to proceed.

"Lean forward on your knees. Lean forward until your forehead is on the floor."

He guided her down, pressing on her shoulders, until her forehead rested against the cold smooth stone and the tips of her breasts brushed against it.

"Turn your head if you wish. If you want to look at me. You may turn your head to the side in this position if you wish to, unless you're being punished."

"Are you going to punish me now?" she asked in alarm.

"No. I may spank you a little, but it's not for punishment's sake."

"Why then?"

"Because it's what I like. Now spread your thighs just a bit. Like this." He pushed her knees apart, pulling up on her hips as she dropped them down instinctively.

"No, keep your hips up high. Arch your back. Open your knees and keep your head down."

When he'd finally positioned her as he liked her, he rubbed her back and took in the view.

"Yes," he murmured. "Beautiful. This is a position I like very much, and I'll want you like this a lot. Do you know why?"

"No." She hid her face, blushing red.

He studied her curiously. "How does it make you feel, Caitlyn?"

"Afraid."

"You mustn't be afraid. I like this position because it means that you're open to me. That your body is available and ready for whatever I may want to do."

"I can't kiss you from this position, though," she pointed out. "I can't take you in my mouth."

"There are other places you can take me," he said after a moment. He put a hand on her bottom to still her trembling limbs. He let one finger slide between her buttocks, to her sensitive little bud. "I'll breach you here, Caitlyn, when you're ready. But you're not ready yet, so I won't do it tonight."

She hid her face in her hands as he caressed her.

"Does that feel good, little one?"

"I'm...I'm...I don't know."

"You're not ashamed, are you? You're not permitted to be ashamed to give your body to me. If you are, I will punish you for it. Do you understand?"

She moaned, drawing her legs together slightly.

"No." His hand landed on her bottom with a slap. "Open, just as I taught you. Your job now is to obey."

"Why?" she whispered. "This is very hard."

"Because when you obey me, it gives me pleasure. When I hold you in my arms, it gives you pleasure, yes? To be close to me, to sleep in my arms?"

"Yes." She sighed. "I love that."

"Well, this is what I love. This is what gives me pleasure, what makes me relax. So if you love me, you'll obey me. Do you understand?"

"Yes," she whispered. He was still fingering her tiny hole, making her squirm and tremble. Then he took both her round buttocks in his hands. He squeezed and caressed them roughly. He spanked one and then the other. She whined softly, but she didn't break the pose.

"Good. Very good. I love that you accepted that without crying or pulling away."

She was still hiding her face.

"Or are you crying, Caitlyn?"

"I'm crying just a little. I'm sorry."

"That's okay. You're allowed to cry." He spanked her again then, a few blows on each cheek, warming her up. Then he stood to pick up his leather belt from the floor.

"Brace yourself, Caitlyn. Don't move."

He gave her a few blows with his belt, nothing too hard. While she jerked a little, again, she didn't move and didn't break the pose. He could hear her mewling behind her hands. He knelt beside her again, rubbing the small of her back.

"Are you being punished, Caitlyn?"

"No," she sobbed.

"Why am I doing this? Do you remember?"

"Because you love to. And because you love me to obey you."

He leaned to kiss her reddened, trembling buttocks, first one and then the other.

"Yes, darling. How quickly you learn. I am very, very proud of you."

* * * * *

In the darkness, Cait snuggled closer to the shelter of his chest. She'd long since stopped crying, but her eyes still felt hot and dry. She didn't know why she'd cried so hard. Nothing he'd done had really hurt, not overly. Not the way it had hurt when he'd spanked her in the orchard.

She supposed she cried because it was a strange and confusing idea, that he wanted to hurt her because that's what he loved to do. And it was just as strange and confusing that she wanted to do whatever he asked of her, no matter how painful, only because he asked. She was desperate to please him because she loved him, and he had told her that he loved her. *He loved her*. For that alone she would do anything, *anything* in her power to make him glad.

"It is hard work, isn't it?" he'd whispered to her afterward as she'd cried in his embrace. "I warned you it wouldn't be easy."

It was hard work but she was determined to please him. It had hurt when he'd worked one finger up into her nether hole, even using the slippery cream he'd produced from a small jar. But she had knelt still and obeyed him even as her face flamed red and her knees trembled with fear.

Someday, he told her, *you'll love the way this feels. You only need to get used to it. We'll practice a little every day, and then one day, you'll be ready to have my cock inside this place...*

No, she wanted to say. No, how could that be, when even his finger had to struggle to get inside?

You must learn to relax. Relax and trust me. It will come, Caitlyn. It will come.

She would learn. She would learn whatever he wanted her to, whatever it was that wives had to do. She would do anything for this man she loved. And she'd get used to this idea of love hurting at the same time love made her want to die from the pleasure and the thrill.

Chapter Eight

Caitlyn was happy to bid farewell to the earl's father in the morning. She couldn't help but sidle behind Duncan as Douglas took his leave, swinging up on his horse with one last glare at her. She knew Duncan didn't like her to cower, but the looks his father gave her made her stomach clench. She couldn't imagine what she'd ever done to make him despise her. But no matter, because Duncan loved her. He told her so.

Every night now, he showed her how much he loved her. Every night now, she fidgeted over dinner waiting for him to put down his cup and look down at her with his deep grey eyes.

"Finished?" he would ask her quietly. She would nod. *Oh, yes, finished. Yes.*

He might as well not have asked *Finished?* but instead, *Are you ready?* Because that was what she heard when he looked down at her at the end of their meal. *Are you ready to come to the bedroom with me? Are you ready to bare yourself to my eyes? Are you ready to do whatever I ask?*

Yes, she was always ready. Always. He would help her from

her chair and the feel of his hot, firm hands on her flesh at last, after a whole day of wanting him, was almost enough to make her eyes close with desire. She thought she would shame herself one day in front of everyone, unable to resist falling to her knees right then and there.

For his part, he would only smile down at her.

He *knew*.

They would hurry up to his bedroom. Sometimes, out of the eyesight of others, they ran, pulling each other along. Sometimes he'd sweep her up in his arms and carry her. Once he tossed her over his shoulder to carry her like a sack, and she'd shrieked with laughter.

The idea that he might drop her never came to mind. She only clung to his surcoat, howling with laughter until he told her, chuckling, to hush. She would do anything for him, and trust him to do anything to her. She knew that he would never hurt her, not in any way she didn't wish to be hurt. Sometimes the things he did were difficult to bear, but she was happy to bear them for him.

Obedience remained the currency between them, every bit as much as laughter and desire and love. In fact, it seemed that the love and desire came directly from the obedience, because the more obedient she was, the more loving he became. The more she learned and understood of him, the closer she felt to him as a wife. She remembered Henna's words to her the first night she'd arrived at Inverness. *It takes time for a marriage to take shape. Time and patience and understanding. And respect.* Truer words had never been spoken. That's why everyone loved Henna, because she was so wise.

It wasn't always easy being obedient. Sometimes she made choices that resulted in being spanked across his lap, or even being stood against the wall to bear strokes from his belt. It angered him most of all if she showed reticence or shame. Sometimes she couldn't help it. Sometimes the things he did to her, the things he demanded of her were so intimate she couldn't hide her unease. But she was learning every night, and she tried hard always to get better. It got easier and more pleasurable with every passing day.

It always began the same, that wonderful moment when they found themselves alone together in his room. He would lock the door and turn to her, watching intently as she took off her clothes and laid them across the chest.

Then he would indicate exactly what he wished of her, tell her very explicitly what to do. Sometimes he would motion her to the bed, order her to lie back and part her legs. Or he might have her lie on her stomach, or kneel and part her legs, and then he would pleasure her with his hands and his mouth. Other times he would snap his fingers and indicate that she was to kneel and take his member in her hands, and kiss and suck him until he released in her mouth. Many times he ordered her to assume his favorite position, kneeling down with her head on the floor, her legs spread wide in vulnerable offering to him.

She would shiver and shudder when he made her wait in that position. And he did, almost always, make her wait, so that when he finally came near and knelt behind her, put his hands on her or pressed his cock to her, she felt something akin to relief. He would use the slippery, scented cream to pry her open between her buttocks in her most private place. She quaked from the terrible intimacy of it, but she soon learned that to cry or balk displeased him and resulted in punishment.

"I'm not hurting you," he would say quietly in warning. "You're hurting your own self. Just do as I say."

And she'd try.

He had teased and trained her over days and weeks, preparing her to take his cock. He let her know the day it would happen, the day he couldn't wait any longer. She sat beside him at dinner that night in tense anticipation. But it had not been so bad. He had been patient and gentle and encouraging and slow. Every time she knelt for him now and leaned forward submissively, and felt him kneel behind her, she remembered how that first time had felt. The hardest part had been letting the large head of his cock in for the first time. It had been terribly painful and frightening. She had tensed and shaken frantically, not believing it could fit.

"No," he had chided. "Do not do this. We worked a long time for this. Open up for me."

His voice had the power to make her do anything, so she had opened as well as she could. And wonder of wonders, he'd pushed just the smallest part of himself inside. And from there, it had happened. At first, she'd been startled by the sharp pain and pressure. But then, all unexpected, she felt a strange and intense pleasure, a fullness such as nothing she'd ever felt in her life. A fullness and connectedness, as he'd pushed deeper inside her. By the time he'd seated himself fully she had moaned despite herself.

She thought, when he took her so firmly and yet slowly in this intimate way, that he could either pleasure her or kill her at will, whichever he chose. The power belonged to him. In the end, that first time, he had pleasured her, as he did every time he now took her from behind. He'd reached around and stroked and teased her until she'd pleaded for release. Then he'd plunged inside her deep and she'd come helplessly, without restraint.

All these things they did each night, and the untold and creative variations of them he demanded left her feeling very content and well-loved. Then they slept, and she drifted into dreams as he cradled her all night in sleep.

Her days, while not nearly as pleasurable, were not so lonely as they'd been before. The smallest children still ran from her, but their mothers smiled and spoke to her sometimes in passing. She grew to know many townspeople by name. She continued on helping Gordon in the garden, and showed some of the older children how to help him too, so the old man's workload was lifted somewhat from his aching back.

Her guards came to soften towards her. She knew by the day of the week who would be with her, and came to know all their names. While they would never address her by name or be overly familiar with her, they did develop an unspoken partnership in crime. They came to understand that, although the earl ordered her to be kept apart from him by day, she desperately wanted to see him. They arranged such "accidents" whenever they safely could. In time, they didn't tell the earl when she asked to venture farther afield than he allowed, and assisted her in some of her crazier schemes.

But he still punished her over the odd scrape. He did find out, somehow, about her riskier adventures. The day she'd gone skinnydipping, he'd come upon her himself. It was a very warm day and her guard had agreed to turn the other way while she took a quick dip in the wooded lake. She made him promise not to look, since she knew she was only to show her body to her husband. She made certain first, of course, that no one else could see where they were.

The water had been so cool and relaxing, she'd stayed in far longer than she should. She imagined she was a mermaid like the ones Erma had spun tales about, with long shining blonde hair and a fish tail instead of legs. She dove under the water, swimming across the lake and back, exhilarated by the feeling of the water caressing her skin. When she'd finally returned to the banks to get out and fetch her clothes, she found Duncan with her gown over his arm. His expression wasn't a happy one.

"Where's Lonnie?" she asked, looking around for her guard.

"Gone," he said. "Sent back in disgrace to spend the afternoon cleaning the stables."

Cait opened and closed her mouth guiltily. "It was my idea."

"Who gets to see your body, Caitlyn?"

"I made him turn around!"

"Answer me, Cait."

"Only you," she murmured quietly.

"Only me. So you know the rule, and yet decided to disrobe and go swimming anyway, just over the rise from a practice field full of sweaty, fighting men."

"But the trees... They couldn't see me."

"Unless they chose to come up here and take a dip on the hottest day of the year."

She blanched. "Did they?"

Chapter Eight

"No, not this time. But it makes me no less angry. I don't know what possessed you to think you might come swim here naked as the day you were born, in front of your guard no less."

"It wasn't his fault—"

"No, it was your fault. But he should have dissuaded you all the same. It's a little late now to have a worry for Lonnie. He'll know better next time after cleaning the stables for a month. And you...I'll have to make sure you won't ever do this again."

"Oh, I won't," she assured him quickly. "I won't. I promise!"

He frowned down at her, unmoved by her pleading gaze.

"What happens when you disobey me, Cait? Remind me."

"You punish me, my lord."

"And do you deserve to be punished for this infraction?"

"Yes, sir," she whispered.

He crossed his arms over his chest. She knew that look well, and she didn't like it. The look when he was considering exactly how he would belabor her tender hindquarters for breaking one of his rules. Sometimes the punishments were almost pleasurable, when she'd committed a smaller offense, when he'd hold her over his lap and give her spankings that playfully stung. From the look on his face, this would not be one of those punishments. This would be one of the punishments that made it hard to sit down for a while.

A few weeks ago, she would have tried to dissuade him, made excuses, begged for pity, but by now she knew it was pointless to waste her breath.

"Come," he said. "Get dressed. Wait in your room for dinner. After dinner, we'll settle this matter."

Oh, no. It was so much worse to have to wait for it, to know it was coming and that it wasn't going to feel good. But she knew it was pointless to try to escape it. She would have to prepare herself for the pain. She thought the swim had been worth it though. With a sigh, she climbed up out of the water and picked her way across the pebbles and rocks on the shore under the stern caress of his gaze.

He shielded her from the direction of the practice field with his tall, broad body while she dressed. She would have rather lain down on the warm, soft grass and let the sun dry her first. She thought that she would have liked to lie down with *him*, and felt his mouth and hands on her skin. She slid him a look, and she thought he was thinking the same thing from the intent, direct way he was looking at her.

"Dress now. I must return to work."

"Someday, might we come swimming here? Alone? You and I? If I wear my shift to cover myself?"

He frowned. "Perhaps."

"I would like to swim with you, Duncan. And then lie down next to you on the shore and let the sun dry our bodies—"

"Dress, Cait." He seemed frightfully agitated all of a sudden. Well, she didn't know why he should be the one all upset. *She* was the one who was going to worry all day about the punishment to come.

* * * * *

Duncan urged her back towards the keep with a firm hand at the small of her back. What he really wanted to do was lead her deeper into the woods, spank her silly, and thrust inside every part of her body that could take him, all in succession, again and again. When he'd seen her come dripping up out of the water like some forest nymph, bare as the day she was born, it had been all he could do not to take her down on the shore.

Sinful. Her body was sinful. He was not a religious man, but her body was sending him to hell every hour of every day. Worst of all, he still wanted, still ached for that which he did not dare enjoy, that welcoming, warm, slick passage that he would not have to take by force. That she was still a virgin didn't escape his thoughts, not for a moment. He wanted to possess her there so ferociously it hurt. But it hurt more, much more, to imagine losing her, and so he held himself in check and availed himself of what he could.

She didn't mind it, didn't even fathom that the ways he used

Chapter Eight

her weren't completely natural. Perhaps they were, in fact, natural and good—they both enjoyed them very much, of that he was certain.

She didn't even balk at his many punishments even though they were, more often than not, trumped up for the smallest, most insignificant offenses, small lapses like being late to dinner or too slow to undress. In this unfairness, she seemed to indulge him. Actually he had a feeling the little sauce enjoyed some of the less severe spankings every bit as well as he.

Then she gave him the occasional opportunity like the present one—an infraction that really called for strict discipline. It had been naughty and downright dangerous for her to go swimming naked in the lake. At the same time, there was something endearing about the hijinks she got up to. A part of him hoped that never changed. If she was perfectly obedient at all times, well, a great part of his enjoyment of life would be taken away.

Somehow he doubted that would ever happen.

He delivered her to her room with a stern reminder to think over her transgression and what she'd do differently next time. As always, he had to squelch the urge to shepherd her inside, lock the door, and rip off all her clothes.

Duties, duties, he reminded himself. He had things to do, places to be, people he had made promises to. Later, at dinner, he felt that same urge to drag her off and have his way with her. He supposed that controlling himself around her was almost as exciting as controlling her. He fixed her with a stare as she skulked across the hall to her place beside him.

"It's a good thing you're not late."

"Why? I'm already to be punished, aren't I?"

He pinched the inside of her arm.

"Little Caitlyn. Do not be too brave."

Not too brave, but brave enough. Brave enough to walk with him down the hall to his room after dinner, but not so brave that she didn't tremble and lag behind. By the time he closed the door behind them she was already awash in tears.

The tears...he loved them and hated them. He watched her

93

undress while they streamed down her face. He thought that it wasn't good for her to be so agitated, that he ought to soothe her. If he was a better man, he would. At the same time, he loved those tears. They showed how anxious she was to please him, to do what he required of her, even though it was going to hurt. Upset, frightened, guilty, ashamed, no matter, she still stood before him and offered her body without pause.

"So many tears, Cait," he said, stroking her cheek. "You would not be in this situation if you'd thought more carefully about your decision to go swimming alone, without permission. Without *clothes*," he added archly.

"I wasn't alone."

"This is not a good time to contradict me, is it, love? Nor a good time to remind me that your guard was there and you elected to bare yourself anyway. It was disgraceful behavior for a modest wife."

"Yes sir," she agreed, sniffling. As he'd taught her, her hands stayed at her side, although he could see she wanted to cover herself.

"You have a beautiful body, Cait. Do you know that? It's far too beautiful to risk showing off where anyone can see it, where any man could be tempted by it. You displeased me greatly."

"I wasn't showing off."

"Enough," he snapped. "If I want to lecture my errant wife without being contradicted every other sentence, I think that's something I have every right to do. Don't you?"

"Yes." She stole a look at him. "I just don't want to be punished. It hurts."

"Well, correction hurts. It has to, or it teaches you nothing. I don't want to punish you severely, but I do what I must. I do it because I love you and I value your safety. You understand that, don't you?"

"Yes."

She understood but she still pouted and fidgeted with a resigned innocence that drove him wild with lust. But there was an agenda here, and fucking her came second. Making her very,

very sorry for what she'd done came first.

"Stand against the wall, Caitlyn. Let's get this over with."

She moved to the wall, facing it. He pushed her shoulders gently.

"Turn around all the way. Present yourself properly. You know very well by now how to do this."

With a sob, she arched her back and stuck her lovely bottom out. *Agenda, punishment, duty,* he reminded himself. *Fucking, in a little while. First things first, damn it.* Her pert little upturned bottom was difficult to resist.

"Your hands," he said.

She placed them in fists against the wall beside her head.

"You are not to move them, you remember."

Her only response was a soft moan. He picked up the special tool he'd secreted up to the room a short while before dinner, the whippy little leather-clad horse crop. He wanted this punishment to be particularly memorable. Not just because he thought she would be ready to take more pain now, and that he wanted her to take more pain than he'd thus far subjected her to. That was only part of it. The other part was that it really had alarmed him to find her stark naked in that pond. His men often went to swim there on warm days. What a scene that would have been.

He tapped the forbidding implement lightly next to her face, against the hard stone wall. God, her thrilling little whimpers made his cock ache. Perhaps he was a sadist after all. But a sadist, if he wanted to, could scar her with a riding crop, break her skin, cripple her, make her bleed, and the very idea of that made him sick. So no, he wasn't an inveterate sadist, just a bit of a scoundrel in his sexual tastes. Fortunately for him, he possessed a wife who indulged him.

Earlier, when he'd decided to use the crop on her, he had swung it against his own thigh and marked exactly which degree of force brought discomfort, which degree brought pain, and which degree brought welts.

"Count, Caitlyn, to twenty."

It was harsh, but he was certain she could take twenty if he started off properly, not panicking her right away by laying them on too hard and too fast. By making her count, he could go by her breath. Her breath would tell him when she was ready for the next blow, and her voice would tell him when it was too hard or not hard enough. He laid the first one just under her left buttock.

She jumped and yelped. "One."

She was crying already, but she was all right.

"Two," she moaned when he caught the other cheek. Three, four, and five made her jump and fidget, and six, the first real blow he gave her, made her break her stance, reaching behind to shield herself.

"Cait, don't be naughty. I haven't been overly strict so far. If you're going to misbehave even now when you're being punished, I'll have no choice but to tie you down and really discipline you severely."

"No." She sobbed and shook her head, shifting from one foot to the other before resuming the correct posture. "I promise I'll be good."

"We'll start again at six, but if you move your hands off the wall, we'll go back to one. Do you understand?"

"Yes sir." Her hands clenched and unclenched next to her ears.

He began again, and she counted. She danced around on her toes and moaned too.

"Breathe through the blows. I know it hurts, but this is to teach you a lesson."

"I know, but it's so hard. Ten! Eleven!" she cried.

She was really having trouble, and he'd only raised a few light welts.

"I think it might be better if I tied you, Cait. For your own good."

She shuddered, sobbing into the wall. "Yes, please."

He removed a thick leather lace from one of his vests. He took Cait's trembling fists in his hands, circling them. He bound her tightly enough to hold her but not so tightly that the blood couldn't reach her fingers. She looked down at his careful ministrations as if they were happening to someone else. He wanted to meet her eyes, to let her know that everything would be okay. It was best if she was tied now, though, because he was going to hit her much harder before the end.

He guided her farther down the wall where a sturdy bolt protruded from the stone.

"Reach up." The leather lace stretched to fit over the top of the bolt perfectly. He pulled at the bonds to be certain they'd hold. They did. With her arms stretched above her, nearly on tiptoe, she was held fast with no recourse to pull away.

Without a word, he resumed her punishment.

"Twelve!" she sobbed.

She arched and pulled at the bonds. Her distress was gorgeous. If he didn't take her down and drive himself into her soon he would shame himself. The sight of her tense back, her shapely buttocks clenching for the next blow was almost more than he could take.

"Thirteen! Fourteen! Fifteen!"

By sixteen she was beginning to scream the numbers through bitter tears, and by twenty she was a very, very punished girl. He had been harsh with her. It was a punishment she wouldn't soon forget. But he wasn't quite ready to release her. He looked at her straining wrists held by the bonds, the red welts rising on her buttocks. No, not yet.

"Caitlyn." He stood right behind her and breathed her name in her ear. She whimpered, turning her head away. "That's all. It's finished." He rubbed her back, testing her arms and shoulders for trembling or fatigue. "Now I want to have you just like this, against the wall, tied up so you can't get away."

She shivered, leaning back to him as much as she could.

"That's what I want, Cait. Do your arms hurt?"

"No," she whispered after a moment, so softly he could barely hear.

He shed his clothes like wildfire. His cock was bursting with need. His hands shook as he threw open the chest to find the lubricant that helped him breach her. He smeared it on his fingers and spread her buttocks open, the lovely bottom he'd wanted to possess all night long. She flinched from his rough handling of her fresh welts. He bit her shoulder.

"I want you. Open for me."

He spread one hand on the front of her hips, using the other to press his cock to her hole. She leaned back against him but he pushed her forward against the wall and drove into her, barely giving her the time she needed to adjust to his thick girth.

But she didn't fight him. No, she was far too well trained for that by now. She yielded to his invasion, sighing and shuddering in his arms. He reached between her legs when he was fully seated, running his hand down her front to press her hard onto his cock. At the same time he caressed and pinched the hidden fold of flesh that made her moan and clench around him. Within moments she was thrashing and pulling at her bonds in the throes of orgasm. The feel of her lithe body bucking against him triggered some animal impulse of his own. He pounded into her and found his own release. He waited, still deep inside her, as the orgasm rolled through him in aftershocks. His hands grasped her trapped wrists. His cock twitched in her tight ass. Her chest rose and fell in soft gasps as he nuzzled her nape.

"Mmm, I have you. You're mine. You're my good girl, aren't you?"

"Yes," she breathed on a long sigh. "Yes."

Chapter Nine

Oh, yes, she was most certainly his good girl, he thought to himself as he released her bonds. He caught her before she slipped to the floor.

"Come and lie down on the bed." He carried her when her legs wouldn't cooperate. "Lie down on your tummy. It will hurt less."

He rubbed her back, looking down at her striped bottom. Yes, she would sit with difficulty for a while, but he'd drawn no blood, and none of the welts were garish. Out of guilt, though, he would let her rest.

"Cait, you did very well." He lay down next to her, pulling her against his body. "I know that wasn't easy to take."

"It was easier after you tied me," she said after a moment. She slid him a look. *Is it okay that I sort of liked that part of it?* her guilty expression seemed to say.

Oh, yes, that's perfect, he thought, smiling back at her. *That means we'll do it again soon.*

She frowned then, suddenly troubled. She whispered, "I really try to be good."

"I know." He kissed her cheek, her lips, her pert nose.

"Do you think...why do you think...why haven't I grown a baby yet? Is it because I'm too bad?"

His brows drew together in a frown. "Who told you about growing babies?"

"Henna. She said when you planted your seeds inside me, a baby would grow. But you've been planting and planting your seeds and no baby is growing. My waist is as flat as it ever was."

"Do you want a baby so badly?" he muttered. "Sometimes they just don't come, no matter how you wish for them."

"I've hoped for a baby. They're so sweet and soft."

His frown deepened. "Babies are a lot of work."

"I'm good at hard work. And I try to be good—"

"It has nothing to do with being good or bad. You're a very, very good wife. I'm sure you'd be a wonderful mother. But there's more to it than that. Sometimes babies...babies are more than you bargained for."

She looked at him sympathetically. "I know you lost your first wife in childbirth. Did you love her very much?"

"Oh Cait." He sighed. What else was there to say? How could he explain if she asked too much?

"I don't think I would die, Duncan. I'm not scared. Henna always says my hips are made for bearing children. I bet I could have lots and lots."

You're not scared, Cait, but I am. I don't want lots and lots. I just want you.

He brushed her hair back from her face, watching the jet black curls fall across his fingers. Would a baby of theirs be white blond like him, or have her hair, dark as night?

"You know," he said, "babies grow when they're ready, not before. Perhaps some day we'll have a baby, but it has nothing to do with how good you are, or how loving, or how kind. You're all of those things, Cait, but it won't make a baby come."

"It won't? Oh. So I just have to wait?"

"Yes, honey, that's what you have to do. I'm sorry.

Perhaps..." He thought for a moment. "If you wanted, you could play with some of the little babies in town."

"They don't like me. They cry when I hold them, and the older babies run away. That's why I need my own baby, because it would love me."

"I love you, Cait. Isn't that enough?"

At the sharp edge in his voice, she looked up at him, mistaking his self-hatred for anger at her.

"Yes," she said quickly. "Of course it is. I'm sorry. I don't know why I can't wait patiently."

He sighed. The world suddenly seemed to him a very bleak place. "Well, go to sleep. It's been a long day for both of us."

Ever obedient, Cait closed her eyes as he covered her up and drew her into his arms. She slept almost immediately, the deep sleep of the innocent, but he was up a long while thinking about what an awful villain he was.

* * * * *

Cait stayed late in her room the next day, partly because her sore bottom made it painful to walk, but more than that, she was despondent about the whole issue of having a baby.

When she'd talked to Henna, she'd made it sound as if a baby would soon be on the way. Duncan made it sound as if it was a remote possibility. It must be difficult indeed to grow a baby if all the seed he'd poured into her hadn't resulted in one yet.

She was still brooding when Henna bustled in with a tray of lunch.

"Dear girl, what ails ya today? Ya look so sad."

"Oh, it's nothing," Cait murmured. "I'm just tired."

"Tired?" asked Henna, perking up. "And sick? Are ya feeling ill at ease when you eat? In the mornings, is your stomach ailing you?"

"No, not really. Why?"

Henna shrugged. "It could be, if you're tired, that you're growing a baby. Have your courses come on you this month?"

"Yes, last week."

"Oh." Her face fell. "Then you couldn't be with child, I'm afraid. That's how you know for sure. Your courses stop."

"No. They've been coming right as rain."

"Well, now...I don't know why...are you still...you and the earl...?"

Cait nodded emphatically.

"That's strange. Well, don't you lose hope."

"Duncan told me babies come when they're ready. It doesn't depend how good or bad you are."

"No, it doesn't depend on that, lass. Duncan's right. If it did, there would be a lot less babies born into this world. If only good people could have 'em."

Cait frowned. "If that was true, I wouldn't ever have been born at all, because my father is awfully bad."

"Is he now?" chuckled Henna. "Your father the king?"

"He's a king, but he was very bad to me. I don't like him."

"And what of your mother, child? What kind of woman was she?"

"A liar and a slut."

Henna gaped, then quickly composed herself. "Oh, I'm sure that's not true."

Cait shrugged. "My father said so."

"And you don't know anything else about her? Your nurse never said anything about your ma?"

"No, ma'am."

"You never asked? You were never curious?"

"I think she probably had very black hair," Cait offered mournfully.

"Oh, dearest," Henna said, leaning down to peck her on the cheek. "You rest now if you're tired. Don't let Henna upset you about where you've come from. What's important is that you're happy now. You are happy now, lass, aren't ya?"

"Yes, of course I am, Henna. And someday, maybe soon, a baby will grow. Then I'll be even happier."

Henna frowned. "Yes, I hope so, lass. Perhaps soon."

Chapter Nine

*****

Henna went in search of him directly. It troubled her very much that the earl's young wife wasn't conceiving, especially when she seemed so disappointed about it.

Well, Henna knew all about women and babies. She would give whatever help she could. Sometimes it was a matter of timing, or a nutritional matter. Perhaps Cait just wasn't eating enough, or getting enough rest.

She found him in the small room off the main hall where he often gathered his men for planning and conferences. At present he was alone—daydreaming, if she didn't know any better. She knocked softly on the half-opened door to gain his attention.

"Yes, Henna. What is it?"

"Am I disturbing your peace?"

"Peace? I have no peace," he sighed, only half joking. "But I have time for you, if you've a problem or concern."

"Well..." Henna began, not knowing exactly how to broach the subject.

"Let me guess, my wife is brooding up in her room again."

"Well, she does seem a little tired today, my lord, and a little woe-be-gone if I do say so."

"We had a late night. A somewhat exhausting night."

Henna reddened. She thought she might as well just come out and say it.

"Why do you think the lass does not conceive?"

Duncan stood up to stare out the window. She detected a slump to his shoulders that wasn't normally there.

"If you're having problems, perhaps I can be of some assistance. There are herbs to use to make it easier to bring on a baby, certain foods that can help, and then the issue of timing—"

"It's not food or timing or any of those things, Henna."

"I know this can be a sensitive issue," the old woman said. "I don't mean to cause you distress. I only want to help."

"She does not conceive because I don't wish it," he blurted

out. "I don't use her that way. I thought you knew that."

Henna's mouth dropped open. "But she said she'd become a true wife to you! Some three months past! And I know for a fact she shares your bed every night."

"Yes, very enthusiastically."

"She said you gave your seed to her, every day!"

"Well, she might learn a little circumspection. Yes, it's true that I do, but only in places that will do her no harm."

"What do you mean, no harm?" asked Henna, narrowing her eyes. "What on earth—"

"Henna, it is none of your business."

"What are you saying? You're using your wife in unholy, unnatural ways, while she remains a...a virgin?!"

"Technically, I suppose she is a virgin, but in general, no, she's no longer very pure."

"Oh, oh..." Henna spluttered in outrage. "I just...I never...I don't believe—"

"She enjoys my attentions as they are, old woman, so don't look so horrified. And she doesn't know any better—"

"No, she doesn't! When you spend in her...her mouth," Henna moaned, "she believes you will plant a baby in her stomach! Poor misguided child—"

"She's not a child! And it's not really my fault she doesn't know, now is it? You're a woman, why don't you teach her the facts of life? Actually," he muttered, reconsidering, "I'd prefer you didn't."

"Oh, you're a smug, horrid blackheart, to use her this way and snicker about it behind her back."

"I don't snicker, nor am I smug or horrid. I'm very happy. We both are, not that it's any of your concern."

"She's not happy. She wants a baby!"

"Yes, I know she does! Believe me, I know it. Don't think this doesn't prick at my conscience every day—"

"And she walks around still a virgin, completely ripe for the taking by any blackguard who might have designs on her. With the king's own blood in her, no less!"

Chapter Nine

"What blackguard? Who wants the king's bastard? She'll bring no power to anyone."

"And what of her mother? Who on earth knows who her mother might be!"

"Some poor victim of the king's and nothing more, surely. Some gentlewoman or whore he forced to spread her legs. He values Cait not at all, so her mother can't be anyone of consequence."

"Really? And yet she's raised in seclusion? Hidden away in a cottage in the woods for seventeen years? Then sent to marry an earl at the edge of Scotland as soon as she's of age, out of the eyes of the countrymen and court? It seems to me you should guard her more carefully."

"I do guard her, Henna! She's guarded all day."

"Then at night, you wrong her, that poor innocent trusting lass. You wrong her and you know it in your heart!"

"How do I wrong her?" he shot back, losing his temper. "Because I try to protect her from the fate that befell my first wife? Because I don't care to see her bleed to death in pain and agony for a fate I selfishly visited on her?"

"Duncan," whispered Henna. "You cannot blame yourself forever. Lenore's death was not your fault."

"How wasn't it, Henna? I was the one who did it."

"It was just that Lenore wasn't built for bearing children. It was an unfortunate accident. It was no one's fault, just a tragedy and a shame. But Caitlyn, she will bear children with ease. I know this, Duncan. I've been a midwife for years. You fret over nothing, over something that is very unlikely to happen."

"Very unlikely, but there is always a chance, isn't there? Anyway, it matters not. All that matters is that I am unwilling to take that chance again. Especially with her."

He left the room, slamming the door behind him. Henna stood still, shaking her head. To think of the earl's young wife being used that way... It made her want to weep for the poor hapless girl. She'd half a mind to steal her away and hide her from him, but she had a feeling the lass would never agree to go.

* * * * *

The first hot day of summer, when the sky was clear of clouds and blue as far as the eye could see, Duncan fetched his wife and told her they were going to the lake to swim. They walked up the rise together hand in hand. Cait practically danced at his side, excited to take the little trip afield.

"It's just a swim, Cait," he reminded her with a chuckle. "I haven't even brought a picnic lunch for us."

"I don't care about a picnic lunch," she said, her eyes shining. "I'm just happy to spend time with you. I never get to see you during the day. And it's so beautiful and warm and pretty today!"

Beautiful and warm and pretty indeed, he thought, gazing at her. She was right. They rarely saw one another in the light of day, only by the darkness of the moon, which seemed appropriate to the dark, strange love they shared. In fact, he felt as if the sunlight burned him, exposed him as the evil man he was, especially in contrast to Cait traipsing along next to him, every bit as bright as the brightness of the day. No day could ever be as lovely, as guileless, as beautiful as she. And he, he was truly the devil—dishonest and deceiving and black in his soul.

"Why do you frown so?" she asked, peering up at him.

He forced a smile to allay her sudden alarm.

"No reason."

Her face fell. "I know you have other, more important things to do."

"No," he said. "That is not it at all, Cait. I promise you have very little idea what I truly think."

Why had he said that? She too forced a smile. He would rather have seen her frown, seen her cry bitter accusing tears, than force that false smile to her face. He'd wanted to do this to give her pleasure, but as usual he was making a mess of things.

"I'm sorry, Cait. I have too many things on my mind that

trouble me, but they are no fault of yours. Don't let me spoil all our fun. Make me smile. Let's while away a few hours at the lake."

He leaned down to kiss her and she seemed somewhat soothed, a soft smile returning to her face. He would have to guard his words around her. She took everything, every frown, every sharp word, every grimace as her personal fault. It had been nearly six months since they'd married, six months since he'd snapped *bring her inside* and turned her his back on her, nuisance that he'd found her. He would have hoped by now she wouldn't feel so unworthy, so unwanted. He knew it was his fault she'd felt that at the start. Surely, she didn't believe he didn't want her now. He wanted her like he wanted nothing else on earth.

But the guilt he lived with...

He hadn't punished her for any infraction, real or imagined, since her illicit foray into the lake, so the memory of that encounter was heavy on their minds, although neither voiced it. He'd felt too guilty to punish her for anything since then, not that she'd committed any crimes of great import. She'd been so obedient since she'd felt the sting of the crop, she was like an angel fallen to earth.

When they arrived at the lake, he stripped nude, but Cait hesitated when she reached her sheer linen underslip. She looked up at him.

"Take it off, you impossible girl. I let it be known to the men that this lake is off limits until late afternoon."

She smiled the small, silly smile that killed him and pulled the filmy garment over her head. Oh, how she looked standing there stark naked and still in the brilliant sun. The pale skin, the perfect breasts, the lovely flared hips that Henna insisted could bear children... The lithe thighs, the graceful way she tiptoed across the rocky shore to the water. And that smile.

He lifted her playfully and tossed her out into the middle of the lake, only because otherwise he'd have started rutting her right there on the shore. She shrieked, laughing, and dived at once under the surface, every bit as comfortable in the water as a fish. They swam and played for some time before he decided he needed to have her in his arms.

He swam to her, taking her around the waist, turning her to face him as they floated in the water, bathed by the blazing sun. It felt incredibly comfortable, and intimate and romantic, all of those things. It seemed in that moment he might have told her everything, every one of his transgressions, and she would have understood in her heart why he deceived her, that he only did it for her own good. In the bright unforgiving sunlight he could have confessed, and she would have smiled that smile and forgiven him. But he stayed silent because he just didn't know how to form the words.

He let things rest as they were, holding her in the water, watching her bob in the circle of his arms. Her knees braced against his thighs. She shifted just a little and wrapped her legs around his waist.

Silly innocent girl. One thrust and he'd be deep inside her, inside that place he denied himself until it drove him mad. He took her waist in his hands, holding her away from his turgid member.

"Even in the daytime?" she teased.

"Always," he sighed, smiling at her. In the water, holding her this way, they were for once face to face. For once he wasn't staring down at her from above as she stood, or knelt, before him. She was so close, so close.

"Perhaps we should get out, lie down for a while on the shore," she suggested. "Look up at the sky. Dry off a bit before you have to go."

I'm not going anywhere. Yes, they would look at the sky together for a while. Perhaps if he stared at the endless blue sky long enough, the future between them would become clear.

They lay on the spongy, warm grass and she put her head on his shoulder, wrapped her leg around his waist. He held her but didn't molest her, wanting to shield her from any accidental eyes. She dozed that way a while, or seemed to, then rose and picked up a nearby stick. He watched her start to draw in the sandy earth. She was so un-self-conscious in her nakedness. He was charmed by the careful way she drew in the sand, the concentration on her face as she bit her lip.

"What are you drawing?" he asked finally, curiosity getting the better of him. He sat up and looked incredulously at the sand.

She smiled at him. She'd drawn a rather involved caricature of her and him and underneath, their names, and a heart, and the eternal lover's question, *Will you love me always?*

The writing was sure, bold, smartly written, even with a stick in the sand. His smile faded.

"Why did you never tell me you could write?"

Her face clouded and she dropped the stick. "I don't know."

"You can read too?"

"Yes," she admitted. "Is that bad?"

"No. But it's unusual," he murmured uneasily after a moment. "Who taught you?"

"My nurse."

"Your nurse. What kind of nurse did you have, to teach you reading and writing? What else did she teach you, Cait? What else can you do?"

She shrugged. "Nothing. I don't know. I only know my letters and a few familiar words. I never read a book. We didn't have any. Are you angry with me?"

Duncan tried to hide the anxiety he was feeling. Henna's frantic words resonated in his mind. *Raised in seclusion? Hidden away in a cottage in the woods? Then sent to marry an earl at the edge of Scotland? You should guard her better!*

It was pointless to question her. He knew she knew nothing of her parents save her unhappy audience with the king. It would only upset her if he brooded upon it, but why on earth would a bastard daughter be taught to read? Why would she be kept so carefully in seclusion? And should he really be worried if she was safe?

"I would have told you. I didn't think it was important," she said, scattering the sand with her foot. Her question, *Will you love me always,* wiped forever from the face of the earth.

I will. I'll love you forever, Cait. I just wish I knew who you were.

She withdrew then into her own thoughts, staring off into the distance. Soon after, with a heavy sigh, Duncan suggested they'd better dress and return to the keep.

Chapter Ten

That night, Cait was shaky in her submission. Duncan knew it was his fault, that he'd been confusing her by demanding wildly varying levels of obedience.

Duncan watched as she dawdled at undressing. Then, as he'd suspected, she chose not to drop to her knees when he indicated she should. Outside the air was heavy and charged. The beautiful blue skies of the day were giving way to gathering storms. Thunder rumbled in the distance as he considered what to do, how to save this situation without harming Cait or driving her further away.

"Are you ill?" he asked, crossing his arms over his chest.

"No."

"You wish to sleep in your own room tonight?"

She bit her lip. "Yes, perhaps." She peered up at him to gauge his reaction to her softly spoken words.

"Why?"

"I don't know."

"Wives are supposed to provide comfort to their

husbands. They are supposed to please them, Caitlyn."

"I know."

"You are supposed to undress in my room and present yourself to me on your knees."

"I know," she whispered again, her eyes shining with tears. Her hands came up to cover her body. "Tonight, I don't want to."

"Very well." Duncan sighed after a long moment. "If that is your choice, it carries consequences. I'll punish you, and then you are free to sleep in your room for one night to consider whether or not to make this choice again."

Her lips trembled and she gave him a look that pained him. Confused, vulnerable, scared. "Do you love me?" she asked.

"Of course I do."

"But only if I do as you say. Only if I follow your commands."

"No." He sat heavily on the edge of the bed. "I love you always, Cait. But I punish you when you don't follow my commands. There's a reason for that, which I've explained to you on many occasions. My rules are there to keep you safe."

"How does it keep me safe to kneel and take you in my mouth?"

His face grew hard. "It does. Believe me, it does."

Silent tears spilled over onto her cheeks. Duncan wished she would just tantrum and scream.

"I thought you enjoyed the things we did together in this room. I had no idea they made you so unhappy."

"I just always thought you loved me. But now I don't know. You frown at me as much as you smile, and you avoid me at all times except when we're in this room."

"I took you to the lake today. We had fun together, didn't we?"

"Until you discovered I knew how to read and write! Then you frowned at me the rest of the day. You always

Chapter Ten

frown at me."

"I frown a lot, Cait. I can't help it. It has nothing to do with my feelings for you. I love you very much. Now come, lay over my lap."

She hesitated. "I don't want to."

"That may be, love, but you'll do it all the same."

"If you love me, why do you hurt me?"

Duncan sighed. "Honestly, we've been over and over this. Do I really need to explain it again? I will if you wish it, but you'll be punished all the same. Now come, let's get it over with."

She dragged over to him, weeping openly now. He pulled her between his legs and tilted her chin up to him.

"These tears, Cait. What are you really crying about?"

"I don't want you to do this. I just want you to hold me."

"Disobedient wives aren't coddled and cuddled, are they? You know that."

He pulled her down over his knee, ignoring her sobbing. Of course he was devastated to see her so upset, but the worst thing he could do would be to let her go now, when she was obviously trying to see where the boundaries lay.

The spanking was harsh and painful, but not angry. He wanted her to feel she was being punished, yes, but to understand that she was loved. Afterward he made her stand again between his legs and look him in the eyes. She was miserable, conflicted, guilty.

"Tell me, Caitlyn, what that punishment was for."

"It was...it was for being...disobedient," she sniffled through her tears.

"For testing me, yes? For purposely not following the rules."

"Yes," she whispered.

"Are you sorry?" She was quiet a long moment. If he had to, he would start all over again.

"I'm sorry I made you angry," she said finally. "I just want you to love me. If I have to be obedient for you to love me, that's what I'll do."

"I told you already," he said, his patience wearing thin, "that I love you always. No matter what you do. No matter if I frown and spend time away from you, you're my wife and I care for you. I won't allow you to be unsafe and unhappy, which is why I require obedience of you. Now repeat it to me, so I know you understand me. Do I love you, Caitlyn?"

"Yes sir."

"And why must you obey me? What is the reason?"

"To...to...to be safe...and happy," she said with a fresh torrent of tears.

"Because I love you and I want you to be safe and happy," he agreed quietly. He hugged her, pulling her close in his arms. "I know you aren't feeling very happy right now, or very safe when I'm hurting you in punishment. Tonight you'll dress and sleep in your own room and think over what I've said. Tomorrow we'll try again."

Her eyes pleaded with his. She didn't want to be sent away, but he knew she needed time to think. She needed to understand the consequences of fighting his system.

"Go on."

He pushed her gently towards her clothes strewn on the floor. She dressed, still shaking with tears. He opened the door to her adjoining room and ushered her inside.

"Do not come back in tonight," he said. "I've told you what I wish."

"Yes sir," she whispered, just as the first hard rain started to fall.

He shut the door and crossed back to his window, staring out at the pummeling storm. Hard lessons now would assure smoother times later, but it still pained him to wish her good night and send her away. He hadn't even enjoyed that spanking, not really. He was more worried about the miscommunication that had caused it. For her to believe he didn't love her...that was the worst thing of all.

Lightning flickered in the distance. Duncan decided to

return to the hall to see if any assistance was needed in preparing for the coming storm. Before he arrived, Connor came striding toward him down the corridor.

"What is it, man? Danger?"

"No, only something you should see. Someone," he amended. "She claims to be mother to Lady Caitlyn."

Duncan took in the uneasy look on his friend's face.

"And who do you think she is?"

"I think she is who she says she is, and much more than that. But she asked to see you and only you, not her daughter. She demanded it," finished Connor with a frown.

"Where is she?"

"In the hall, my lord."

"I'll meet with her alone—"

"Duncan," Connor warned.

"I'll meet with her alone! And see that Cait doesn't enter the hall without my permission," he added as an afterthought.

Duncan stalked toward the great hall. He'd have answers now, at long last, from this woman claiming to be Cait's mother, as if anyone like she had the right to call herself a mother. Abandoning her daughter to be raised like a pauper in the woods, alone with an aged nurse and a king for a father, and no earthly knowledge of who she was or of anything of the world.

He banged open the door, worked into full fury, but stopped still as she turned eyes on him that were exact replicas of Cait. The woman drew herself up haughtily.

"You may think of me whatever you wish, bold warrior," she intoned at his expression, "but you will hear my words before you send me away."

Cait's mother. Duncan had no doubt she was exactly who she claimed to be. To say that she resembled Cait was an understatement; it was as if Duncan looked upon Cait herself in twenty or twenty five years, garbed in the woad robes of a priestess. *A priestess.* She resembled Cait in appearance, but that was all. For this woman, though petite, had a presence that dwarfed Duncan and made him stop short where he was. A presence that Cait did not in any way possess.

A priestess. A high priestess of some kind, if not the *highest* priestess, he thought suddenly. He had known there was more to Cait's parentage than he had been told, and now it was explained. As he thought all this the woman glared back at him balefully, looking down her nose at him with a frown. She was dressed in a plain, unassuming gown, but exuded such a strange and affecting power that she might as well have been garbed in the richest, most rare of dress with bedazzling jewels. He blinked, breaking her stare, suddenly certain that she tried to bespell him. Perhaps, he thought belatedly, he should not have met with her alone.

"I have been on a merry chase about Scotland looking for my daughter," her voice rang out, "and I find her here at Inverness Keep, in the Devil's own hands." She glowered at him as she spoke the last words.

"I am no devil, madam," returned Duncan, "but I have some words for what you are, to have cared for your daughter as you have."

Her eyes narrowed, sizing him up. "You might do better to address me with respect. Do you know to whom you speak?"

"I have an idea of your high station, but I speak to you as the mother of my wife. The absent, careless mother," he added with a scowl.

Her sudden peal of laughter surprised him. "Oh, cry and wail. My daughter was well cared for, better cared for that I left her alone. You understand me, Devil?"

"My name is Duncan of Inverness."

"And my name is Edana, high priestess of the Isles, lest we both get confused. Now that the introductions are out of the way perhaps we can speak plainly and clearly. If you are finished criticizing my maternal capabilities, that is."

Duncan stood and watched her with his lips pursed in a

frown. "Plainly and clearly sounds fine to me. What is it you want?"

Edana lifted her chin and stared at him as lightning flickered in the darkened hall.

"For all you imagine I have no maternal feelings for my daughter, the truth is I have traveled here to see that she is well."

"She is well," Duncan said. "For all that I am named a Devil, I am a loving husband to your daughter Cait."

"Love?" said Edana, her brows lifting. "Is it so? My lucky daughter, then, to know that which her mother has not."

"Yes, lucky," Duncan agreed. "We live very happily here. She is safe and content and much loved."

"I am happy to hear it," said Edana, her voice finally softening. "Based on your unfortunate moniker, I must say I expected the worst. But she is not completely safe here. You must hear this and know it, and take it to heart."

"What do you mean? She is very safe here. She has a guard. She is always supervised. I know she is not one to be careless with. She has the blood of the king...and you..."

"Yes, me. Wretched pagan blood. The blood of a priestess who bore her with a king from the Beltane fires. I'm a poor mother, but I do have some worth to her. I have seen danger for her and I come to warn you. There is danger in a man—"

"I promise you, lady," interrupted Duncan indignantly, "she is in absolutely no danger from me."

"I know it," she snapped. "I know much more than you can ever hope to know. I tell you only what comes to me, and what comes to me is a vague feeling that my daughter is not secure. There is a sinister specter I can see just in the corner of my thoughts."

"The king. It's the king you see. She claims that he hates her, that he wants her dead."

Edana laughed. "The king? No, I know the king. I hold

his soul in my hands and I feel what he feels and know what he knows. She is in no peril from him. No, this threat is unknown to me and as such, I come to warn you to look after her carefully."

"Madam, I already do. I do everything I can, everything in my power to protect her."

"Do you?" she said, looking at him with a searching look that set his hair on end.

"Yes, I do," he replied with a little less conviction. "I protect her better than you have, at any rate."

"Do you dare to judge me, bastard earl, Devil, living here at the edge of the earth?"

Duncan's eyes flashed fire, accented by a deep sudden boom of thunder. "I'll thank you not to insult me in my own home, madam. I am your daughter's husband—"

"And I am her mother! And despite your judgments and accusations, I care very much for my child!"

The weight of guilt was apparent. Even her priestess powers and attitude couldn't hide the sadness behind her eyes.

"Why then?" he asked suddenly, softly. "Why did you abandon her? Let her grow up unwanted and alone?"

"Why? You might as well ask me why the sun rises in the sky and the waves fall on the shore. It is the way of my world. Her father's blood taints her, as much as I wish it wasn't so. I had high expectations for her, but she is too cowardly and retiring to come after me and reign as high priestess."

"Cait is exceptionally brave," protested Duncan over the din of the suddenly violent storm.

She frowned. "In some areas, perhaps. But not in the areas that matter. She has no power, no insight, no inner or outer strength. For those reasons I am sure she is quite the biddable wife to you, but she is completely useless to me."

"Useless. What endearing terminology for a mother to use to describe her own daughter. Perhaps it is best that she knows you not at all."

"I hid her away because I couldn't stand for a daughter of mine to be raised at court. That was a mercy done for her, for her protection. It was a kindness above all kindnesses."

"Kinder still to know her mother's love."

"Ah, but she knows a husband's love now," she mocked. "And is that not enough?"

As if on cue, Cait's voice, soft and plaintive, sounded from the doorway. "Duncan?"

"Cait, don't come in here."

She rushed to him and threw herself into his arms before Connor could stop her.

"Duncan, the storm! Please let me stay with you. I'm afraid!"

Duncan looked over her shoulder to where her mother watched, hunched down, almost completely obscured in the shadows of the corner. How had she gotten there so fast? How could she make herself disappear in plain sight? She watched him, and watched her daughter too, missing no detail.

"Cait." He felt suddenly desperate to have her away from Edana. "Go to Henna. Henna will sit with you through the storm."

"I'm sorry!" she whispered. "I'm so sorry. I'll kneel for you. I'll please you. I'll do whatever you want. Please! Please give me another chance, Duncan. Don't make me sleep alone! I'm sorry!"

His face grew hard at her words. In any other circumstance he would have taken her to his room and not let her go for hours, but right now, right now...

"I...you...I told you why we must sleep apart tonight. If the storm frightens you, you must go to Henna. I've duties I must see to tonight. Now go," he said, throwing a look at Edana. He didn't care for the way the woman watched her. "Go, now. Obey me. This is for your own good."

With one last sob she let him set her firmly away.

"Connor," he snapped, guiding her to the door. "Take her to Henna, and have Henna take her to her room and keep her there." He emphasized the last three words.

When Cait was gone, Edana emerged from the dark corner, once again the haughty high priestess.

"How happy and content she looks," she said acidly.

"She does not like the storm."

"And how kind and affectionate you were when you pushed her away."

"I didn't want her to see you. I was trying to get her away. I do not trust you at all."

"Perhaps it is best if you do not." She looked thoughtful then, tilting her head at him with a puzzled expression.

"How long have you been married? She does not breed?"

"No," said Duncan tightly. "She is not yet with child."

"You have not even had her," Edana scoffed, her suspicions confirmed by the flush of his cheeks. "Why is that? Are you a catamite, perhaps? Do you have difficulties with your organ? I can offer some herbs and remedies if you wish."

"I have no difficulties, madam."

"She is not so biddable then as I thought," she said in surprise. "Well, perhaps she has some of my blood in her after all." She looked thoughtfully at the door through which Duncan had sent her away. "If she is still a virgin, if you've no use of the girl, I'll take her. I'll harbor her at Canna Isle and she'll come to no harm."

"No," said Duncan. "She is mine and you will only remove her from me if you put me, and every man who fights for me, to the sword. But long before then, lady, I will destroy you, if you think to take that which is mine."

Edana's eyes widened. "I do not fight with swords, I assure you, Duncan. And these are strong words from a man who cannot even be bothered to bed the woman in question."

"In due time," was all he replied.

Edana fell silent then, and pensive.

"There is no time. You must make her your wife in truth. Only this can subvert the danger that threatens."

"You speak nonsense."

"I speak truth!" she insisted. Her face changed, became so stark that Duncan grew alarmed.

"What is it? What do you see?"

"I do not know. An incomplete vision. An unexpected direction that must be avoided. You must get her pregnant with all haste."

"I don't believe you. I don't believe in your pagan visions and lies."

"Why are you frightened then, if you don't believe? Let me take her if you can't or won't see to this. Let me take her to a safe place where she can be protected and hidden away."

Protected. Hidden away. How much did he love her? Enough to let her go? Was Edana telling the truth about Cait being in danger? Or was she only trying to prise her daughter away from him using vague veiled threats?

"If I make her pregnant, this mysterious 'danger' you speak of will be averted?"

"I can't say. It appears to me that it is so."

"My first wife died," he blurted out. Why on earth had he said that to her?

Edana looked at him sharply. "Died? In childbirth?"

For a moment, a soft expression of sympathy flitted across her face. "And you think to protect my daughter from the same fate?"

"Yes. I hoped to."

Edana drew a deep breath, and her gaze met his. She stared at him for a long while.

"Have no fear," she said finally in a low voice. "Even a brutish man such as you cannot get a child on her she won't be able to bear. She will have the talent of her mother, her grandmother, and her great-grandmother to bear children with ease."

Duncan rubbed his face and frowned. How could she

know that? The disembodied way she stared at him made his hair stand on end.

"You don't believe me, but I know it to be so. So I warn you, Devil, delay no further in putting this innocent to the 'sword.' If you do not, I will consider again if she might, after all, suit my own purposes. A virgin such as she can be a valuable asset and bargaining tool."

"You will bargain with my wife's virginity over my dead body."

"See to it, then, that it is quickly gone," replied Edana in warning before she turned, and without another word, took her leave.

Chapter Eleven

Duncan took the stairs two at a time, half frightened, half enraged. He had one thought and one thought only hammering in his brain. *Cait. Cait. Cait. Cait.*

I will consider again if she might, after all, suit my own purposes. He took it for the veiled threat it was. He had seen Edana looking at Cait, reconsidering, plotting, softening towards her. Priestess or no, he would kill her with his own hands before he'd let her take Cait away. He walked down the hall towards her bedroom and worked to school his face to calm. He knocked softly and was chagrined to see Henna open the door.

"My lord, she sleeps."

"Wake her then."

Henna slipped out into the hall, whispering insistently.

"She has retired for the night. She sleeps!"

"Well, then, she shall wake. Let me by—"

Henna put her hand on his arm.

"You'll not take her to that woman. Mother or not, I don't trust her. I didn't like the look of her."

"I assure you I have no intention of that. Let me pass."

"Why? What will you do to her now? She cried herself to sleep after you sent her away!"

Duncan gathered his last hold on his temper to speak civilly. "Henna, I love you dearly, but I promise if you do not let me pass to my wife at once you will live with regret."

Henna set her face and stepped aside. "What is it?"

"It cannot wait, Henna. Not any longer. I'm sure you'll be pleased to hear that."

"You'll have her tonight?"

"Yes, right now."

"In this temper, this agitation? My lord—"

"Henna, I beg you, please. I don't wish to hurt you in anger," he said, pushing her from the door.

"Better me than her. You've made her cry enough already!"

Their escalating voices roused Cait, who sat up in bed in alarm. Duncan pushed past Henna and lifted Cait from the nest of rumpled bedding, carrying her over to the door between their rooms and kicking it open with a bang.

"My lord—" Henna pleaded.

"Good night, Henna," said Duncan before slamming the door. He dropped Cait on the bed and began to shed his clothes. She watched for a moment in wary confusion before standing to take off her own clothes. Before she could fall to her knees he took her arm and led her back to the bed.

"I'm sorry," she said in a whisper. "I'm sorry, Duncan, for whatever I did."

"Hush." He lay down next to her on the bed. He traced her arm, looking down at her black curls, her striking pale blue eyes.

Little priestess. It was all explained. No wonder she cast such a spell on him.

She peered up at him nervously. "What can I do to make things better? Tell me. I'm sorry, earlier tonight—"

He put a finger to her lips. "Hush. Earlier tonight was an eternity ago. You're forgiven. Now, you must forgive me for being untruthful to you."

Chapter Eleven

"You were untruthful to me?"

You have no idea how terribly untruthful I've been.

"There is another way to...to make a baby come," he said, "but I...I haven't wanted to use you that way because...it will hurt the first time."

He looked down at her to gauge her reaction to his ridiculous excuse. She was not an idiot. She knew as well as he that he hurt her, at least a little, every time he forced her from behind, or made her lay over his lap, or stand against the wall to be punished. She made the obvious assumption, that what he was talking about would hurt even worse.

"I...I..." she stammered bravely.

"It will not hurt as much as you think. It will hurt just a little in the beginning and then it will feel fine. Quite wonderful actually. I'm not sure why I waited so long to show you this."

Perhaps because I was afraid you might die.

"Will it feel good for you too?" she asked, no doubt because of the scowl on his face.

"Yes, dearest, it will feel good for me too."

"Then why do you look so sad?" She reached up to caress his face, soothing him with her soft, warm touch.

"I just feel anxious. Anxious to get it over with." He parted her legs, reaching between her thighs to caress her center. How many nights had he lain awake dreaming of this? Even now he was so hard it was painful.

"Don't worry," she said. "I won't be mad if you hurt me."

He couldn't help but smile as he nuzzled her.

"God forbid I would hurt my precious wife."

"Oh." She sighed as he found her sensitive button and pinched it, then stroked it lightly. "That feels good." She arched against him. It was an invitation he would no longer deny.

He nudged his cock into her slit slowly, feeling its wet welcoming heat.

"Oh, that feels...different," she breathed.

He sighed, arching over her, sucking her nipples into his mouth gently, then biting just enough to make her gasp. "Oh, please!"

"Please what?" he asked, finding it difficult to speak.

"Please hurt me now. I'm ready," she said, wrapping her arms around his neck.

* * * * *

Oh, it felt good, but she knew something painful was coming. He'd warned her. She just wanted to get it over with. His strong arms cradled her and she knew it was coming. She tensed as he rose up between her legs. He drew her thighs farther apart, positioning herself with a low moan, and then he thrust in her, rough and deep.

She tensed and gasped at the pain of it. Her nails dug into his back, but he didn't move, he didn't release her.

"Be easy, Caitlyn. That's the worst of it."

She lay very still under him.

"Okay? It will start to feel better in a moment."

"I'm okay," she said, but she was anything but. He had forced her open with a terrible sharp pain she'd never felt before, as if something had torn.

"I think...I think I'm broken."

He chuckled softly. "I promise you're not."

He nuzzled her for a moment, easing in and out of her with shallow, slow movements. To her surprise, it did begin to feel good. Exceptionally good. The sharp, jagged pain of his entrance eased into something much more exciting and deep.

He seemed to sense the moment she relaxed, the moment her sigh signaled the desire for something more. He thrust in her deeply then, to the hilt, cradling her, pulling her closer, closer still. Her bottom was still painful from the punishment she'd had earlier. She felt his fingers grasp her welted buttocks, adding an edge of sharp sensation to the liquid, shapeless pleasure overtaking her, washing over her. He was so *close* to her, so very close.

This was nothing at all like when he'd taken her with his

mouth, not at all the same, and it was strikingly different from when he'd taken her in her bottom. Then, he had been slow, careful, deliberate, bent over her back, taking her with tense and measured strokes. Now, he almost lifted her from the bed with his powerful thrusts, and she arched to take more and more of him. Each time he filled her, exquisite, beautiful sensation warmed her entire pelvis and shot up to her tingling breasts. His lips were buried in her neck, in her hair, next to her ear.

"Oh, Cait, Cait, Cait..." he whispered as he took her. She could only moan in reply. She was so full, so warm, so completely close to him. She could see now how a baby might come of this. There had to be an extra power, an extra potency to this kind of joining. She had never felt something so magically akin to *love*. "Duncan, please," she sighed, pulling him closer.

"Yes," he agreed. "Yes, yes, yes."

He loved her until she almost sobbed from the arousal that gathered at her core. With a flash of white heat, she came, molten love and lust overtaking her body, and shuddered through a long, glorious orgasm in his arms. He came too, arching over her powerfully and grunting as he emptied his seed inside her. With a long, drawn out sigh, he came to rest.

He collapsed beside her, then stroked her arm and shoulder thoughtfully. Cait looked up at his morose expression in puzzlement. She had greatly enjoyed this joining, even considering the initial pain. It had been a small price to pay for the pleasure that followed, but Duncan looked down at her as if he mourned.

"Are you sad?"

"No." He forced a smile, with effort, to his face.

She wished she knew why he was so unhappy. Ever since their trip to the lake, ever since she'd written in the sand...

"Duncan, if you wish it, I will never read and write again. If it displeases you... I do not care if I do it or not."

He shook his head. "Cait, no...I don't care either. Listen, I wish I could explain... Things are just complicated now. Things grow more complicated by the day. But it's no fault of yours, I promise you. My happiness does not hinge on whether my wife can read or write, but on whether or not she is safe."

"Am I not safe?" she asked. "I stay with my guards, Duncan. I won't stray into town if you don't wish me to."

"You are safe. There is no need to worry if you continue to follow my rules. Now, you must be tired, dearest," he said. "Close your eyes and sleep."

"I'm not tired," she said, but she knew her limp, relaxed body cradled against his said otherwise.

"Oh, aren't you?" His fingers began to move lazily over her belly. "My little reader. Let's play a game. I'll trace letters on your skin, and you tell me what I write."

"Okay. But what if I am wrong?"

"Then there will be a forfeit to pay. So listen well."

"Listen? As you trace on my skin?"

"Listen. Concentrate with your body. I won't repeat any letters," he warned.

"Okay. I'm ready."

He began to trace the first letter on her stomach. She shivered at the ticklish sensation.

"Be still," he said, fighting a smile.

He traced what might have been an X or a K, but Cait thought surely it must be a K. An I, that was easy enough, and then an S and another S. She licked her lips in expectation. He traced an M and then an E.

"What did I spell, wife?"

"Kiss me," she answered with a shy smile.

"Gladly," he replied, kissing her soundly. "But tell me now, what did I spell?"

She giggled. "Kiss me."

"Oh, you are a greedy one." He sighed, kissing her again, this time more deeply. "But what did I spell?"

"Duncan, you—" she began, but he cut her off with a teasing *tsk*.

"No, I didn't spell Duncan. Incorrect. Turn over and receive your penalty."

Chapter Eleven

With guilty pleasure, she turned her back to him. He landed a glancing blow on one buttock, and then the other.

"You are an unfair master."

"Perhaps. But you are a naughty pupil. One who sometimes enjoys punishment too much."

"I think I'm not alone in that," she commented drily, which earned her another sharp smack.

"All right. Another word." He kissed and blew warm breath on the small of her back. "This time on a more sensitive area. Surely you'll feel this with great accuracy."

"I'm ready," she said, squirming.

"Don't try to distract me with your charms, wench," he laughed. His fingers began to brush over the surface of her rounded buttocks.

Her eyes narrowed. "What...I cannot..."

"I haven't started yet. Just lie still and let me touch you as I wish."

"Yes, Duncan." She relaxed as he caressed her and soon began to probe her intimately.

"Oh... Oh, Duncan..."

"Mmm," he rumbled, nuzzling her. "Pay attention. You're distracted, wife."

"You're distracting me." She squeaked as he breached her in both places with his fingers at once.

He drew one finger, wet with her dew, from between her legs and began to write on her left buttock. "Listen," he whispered.

He drew an O she easily recognized, then a B which she had to concentrate hard to figure out, then an E, and the Y she expected. The M and E she expected too, and she moaned.

"Yes, Duncan. I will. Whatever you wish. What do you wish?"

"Part your legs wider." He pushed her down to the bed, coming over her back. His teeth closed on the back of her neck as he positioned his cock between her legs. Looking down, she saw the blood that remained from their earlier joining and it made her shiver with desire. She was his now, undeniably, indelibly his. His true wife. If she grew heavy with his child, it would be even more evident. She desperately craved for it to be so.

* * * * *

The next weeks were busy as the town and keep made preparations for winter. Cait tried to stay out of Duncan's way, although they met as always at night in his bedroom. His lovemaking was as rigorous and thorough as ever. She grew to love the new way he took her, when he held her so close and thrust in her so deeply she thought she would die from the pleasure. When he used her that way, she felt closer to him than ever, although afterwards, he often looked back at her with a frown.

But she didn't mind. She was happy and she knew he loved her, and that was her only care.

Cait walked across the sand, having escaped to the beach for the day. She loved the fall air, the cooling temperatures and soothing ocean breezes. The beach was somewhat remote, but her guards let her visit it when she wished. She suspected Duncan might disapprove. She never asked his permission since he might expressly forbid her to go. If he knew how many gowns she'd ruined scurrying down the rocks to reach the small stretch of beach that could be walked upon, he would certainly punish her and forbid her to return.

Today, unfortunately, she had ruined another one. Even more unfortunately, she ran into Duncan and Lord Douglas while returning to the keep to change.

"Well, look here," Lord Douglas cried. "Princess Ragamuffin is back from her playtime. Really, son, it boggles me that you let your wife comport herself in this fashion. Look at her gown."

Annoyance at his father warred with true chagrin on Duncan's face. Cait could see he was displeased.

"Where were you, Caitlyn?"

"I'm sorry," she said, trying to brush away the worst of the sand and dirt. "I have others. I was just returning to change."

"I don't care about the dress," he said impatiently. He knew she had trunks full. He'd ordered them all for her himself. "Where have you been? On the rocks?"

"Down on the beach," she admitted. "But Desmond was with me. I didn't go near the water. Isn't it okay? I love to walk on the shore."

She felt so forlorn and ashamed that he might be unhappy with her. She had done something she knew he would disapprove of, and now embarrassed him again in front of his father.

"You may walk on the beach if you wish," he finally said. "But you must take better care of your belongings. Not every woman is so fortunate to have gowns such as yours."

"I know." She bowed to him submissively. "Through your kindness."

"Yes, through my kindness. You'll take better care of them or you'll be punished."

"Yes sir," she said. Lord Douglas watched the whole exchange with narrowed, mocking eyes. Horrible man, she thought. She hoped he would not be around for very long this time.

* * * * *

As Cait made off for the keep with Desmond at her heels, Lord Douglas fell into step beside Duncan.

"I don't know how you allow such impertinence—"

"Father," Duncan interrupted, holding up his hand. "She's my wife. My problem. No concern of yours."

"And this wife is the one who will bear my family line?"

Duncan snorted. "Family line. Such as it is, when you call me your bastard."

"Bastard or no, you have been a good son to me and brought much pride to my name with your service to the king. I would not see my grandchildren brought up by an addled woman such as she. They'd be lucky to survive infancy."

Duncan gritted his teeth. He had no idea why his father disliked Caitlyn so much, except perhaps that he disliked and disapproved of everyone—everyone, that is, except himself.

"Caitlyn will be a fine mother. I'm sure that will shortly be proven out."

"Shortly? It's been months since you've married and she's not breeding yet, is she? I sincerely hope not, if she's scaling over cliffs to cavort on a beach with the blessing of her husband. Alone with those boys you set to guard her."

"Boys? Desmond and the others are some of my most valued soldiers. He's young, but he's responsible and capable, just as the others are."

"Capable," laughed Lord Douglas. "I know how capable young men like that are. All the more surprising that you let them accompany your wife alone to these secluded haunts of hers."

It was Duncan's turn to laugh at his father's outrageous suggestion. To imagine his shy, obedient Cait offering herself to her solemn-faced guards, or to imagine his most trustworthy men betraying the leader they worshipped. It was ludicrous.

"Father, believe me. There is no doubt in my mind that when she finally breeds, the child will be mine."

"Your mother was a high placed woman who stepped out on her husband."

"Yes, stepped out on him with you. My guards have more honor," he muttered under his breath.

Douglas pretended not to hear that cutting remark, although Duncan could sense him ruffling with rage. "Well, she's your wife. If that's how you choose to govern her."

"Yes, she is my wife," Duncan snapped.

Henna, Edana, even his father had endless opinions on his treatment of her, endless judgments about something that was none of their concern. "She is my wife, *my* wife, and belongs to none other, so I'll do as I see fit, father, now and for the rest of my life. I'll thank you to remember that."

Chapter Eleven

"As you wish," said Lord Douglas tersely. "You may do as you wish with your wife."

* * * * *

You may do as you wish with your wife. Yes, his foolish son could do as he pleased, but Douglas would do as he pleased too. He would have to take the girl and take her soon. Beat her, fuck her, debase her, whatever he could do to her. Seeing her again after several weeks had dampened neither her allure nor his desire.

Unfortunately, he couldn't just lay hands on her. His son was overly fond of her, that he could tell. He coddled her. She would run to him at once the moment Douglas hurt her. Figuring out how to guarantee her unwilling silence would take planning and guile. No matter. He would put his mind to it. He would figure it out. A man as immoral and depraved as he would have no problem trapping the girl. He would make it work out so she was the one who burned with guilt and self-hatred for what he did to her, even though he would be totally to blame.

Chapter Twelve

That night, upstairs in the bedroom, Cait bared herself for her husband with downcast eyes. A small sound and gesture had her kneeling before the fire in the submissive posture he liked, the posture she often assumed when punished. He took off his thick belt and doubled it over in his palm.

He wasn't in the mood for offering reprimands or stern words. Sometimes he felt like lecturing his wife, but other times he simply felt like disciplining her. This was one of those times.

He wasn't even sure why he disciplined her. She was a tomboyish rapscallion on her best days. She climbed trees and scaled rocks as much as she played the sedate mistress of the keep, so ruining her gown was hardly cause for punishment. He suspected he disciplined her this night out of frustration with his father, and with some messy politics to the north that were going to need his attention soon. So be it. She submitted to whatever he decided to dish out, deserved or not.

He felt the familiar powerful arousal as he began to punish his wife. She jerked at the stinging contact of each blow. He was slow, intentionally making her wait for each stroke. He didn't make her count out loud.

She was crying by the end, trembling in her effort to hold her pose, to not collapse on the floor to escape the belt's blows. She rarely did that because it only brought her more. Still, he said nothing to her, neither encouraging nor chastising. He felt in a strange mood. She too seemed ill at ease. He knelt behind her, stroking his fingers up her back, then down between her legs.

"Caitlyn," he sighed.

She was silent. He pulled her hips up and pressed his cock to her bottom. He still took her there quite a lot, most often after she was punished, but sometimes just because he wished it. She moaned as he thrust his fingers into her, easing the way. She barely resisted now. She was open and waiting, and he thought it was the most beautiful thing, to feel her unresisting acceptance of him.

He pressed into her, leaning over her back, breathing down the delicate curve of her neck. She sobbed now, not because he hurt her, he knew, but because she thought she had been bad and that he was still punishing her.

"Caitlyn, enough." He put his arms around her and thrust in her deep as she quaked under him. "I love you, Cait. I truly do."

But when he finished and withdrew from her, she was still tearful. He slid his thumb across her cheeks, gently brushing them away.

"I have told you it's enough, sweet. What ails you?"

"I don't know," she cried. "I feel so emotional. I...I...I know it's awful to say, but when your father is here...I'm afraid."

"Afraid?" he said. "You don't need to be afraid of a mean old man. Don't let him upset you."

"I know he's your father, but I don't like him. I hate him," she said with something like terror in her eyes.

"Oh Cait. Hush. Hush now." He rocked her in his arms before the fire.

"Are you angry that I hate him? I try to be respectful, but I can't...I can't..."

"I'm not angry." He silenced her with a finger upon her lips. "I'm not angry with you at all. I'm just as annoyed as you that he's here. And there's some trouble that might draw me away from home for a bit. I tell you truthfully, Cait, I don't want to go. I don't want to leave you." He dropped a gentle kiss on her upturned lips.

"You'll leave me?" Her voice trembled.

"Just for a short while."

"For how long? How long will you be gone?"

"A few weeks. No more than two, most likely. You'll be safe here."

"And will you be safe? Will you come back to me?"

"Of course I will, dearest. How could I not? Come, you're overtired. All this crying. It tires me just to watch you. Come to bed and let me help you relax."

And he did, spreading her wide on the coverlet and lowering his mouth to her most intimate, sensitive core. At first she still sobbed and shuddered, resisting, but he would not be denied. He loved her, caressed her with his lips and tongue until she began to relax. He teased and explored her with his mouth until she gasped. He felt the orgasm when it shook her. She bucked against him, crying out, then closed her eyes, exhausted and still. He let her rest, lifting her and moving her over just enough to climb beside her into bed.

"Don't leave me," she whispered just before she drifted off. "Please keep me safe."

"I will always keep you safe, you know that." But he lay awake a long time worrying about her after her eyes closed.

* * * * *

She couldn't bear it. She couldn't bear for him to leave her. If he died, if he did not return, she would be lost again, abandoned and alone. It was simply too awful to think about. She knew he was strong and capable, and defended by many brave men. But he was also an earl, and the forests were dangerous.

Chapter Twelve

She felt so miserable. Her emotions were all over the place. She dreamed every night of being alone and friendless again, and awoke in the mornings nauseous with dread. She didn't feel right at all. Even when the morning queasiness subsided, she felt like crying and laughing in the same moment, and she had the strangest thoughts and emotional feelings. Just looking at a beautiful shell or a pretty sunset could make her start bawling.

Now, cradled in his warm, cozy embrace, she tried to let all of that fall away. *My husband loves me. My husband loves me.* The mantra that protected her from everything. As long as she was in his arms, everything would be all right.

But the next morning he was gone. She jumped from the bed in alarm, dressed more quickly than she ever had in her life, and ran to the courtyard with Lonnie, her guard, calling after her to slow down. But no, Duncan wasn't gone yet. He was there helping the men prepare for the journey. She ran to him, nearly getting run over by a horse.

"Cait!" he barked, pulling her to safety. "Watch out!"

"I thought you left already." She threw her arms around his neck. "I thought you left me without saying goodbye."

"We leave tomorrow. And you will not become frantic over it," he said, noting the tears in her eyes. "Do you understand me? I won't have sobbing and hysteria." He made her look into his eyes, and made his voice hard and stern. "You will not fall apart over this. Wives let their husbands go, and they trust them to come back."

"But what if...what if..."

"No what if's. The only 'what if' is what will happen to you if you don't obey me," he said so only she heard.

She blushed under his gaze. She was still tender from the night before.

"You won't leave me without saying goodbye?"

"I certainly won't." His eyes swept down over her figure and back up to her face. "You will have quite the goodbye tonight, dearest, believe me. Now go," he ordered, gently nudging her away. "Keep busy, go and do something. Dig in the dirt or scale rocks or trees or whatever uncouth activities you normally do throughout the day."

Cait turned to go reluctantly, and whispered "As my husband commands."

* * * * *

That night at dinner Cait had little appetite. Duncan scolded her and insisted she eat more than she really wanted to. Eventually he resorted to feeding her the choicest bits of food from his own plate.

"You'll need your energy, wife," he reminded her under his breath.

She loved when he looked at her that way, and spoke to her in that husky, suggestive voice. It was a *devilish* look, she thought with a smile. She remembered when she'd first learned she was to be wed to the Devil of Inverness. How alarmed she'd been! It seemed silly now to think back about it. No, the only devil she knew was Lord Douglas. Even now he glowered at her over his cup. She kept her eyes averted from the horrible old man and his icy cold stare. Even his freezing gaze couldn't cool the flush that arose on her cheeks as she felt Duncan's hand roving over the top of her thigh to rest at the juncture there.

"Duncan," she protested, putting her small hand over his. "Not here."

He pretended not to hear her, and did not remove his hand, only widened his smile.

"Are you finished, wife?"

Yes.

Hand in hand they retired down the hall to the stairs and up to the chamber they shared every night. Cait was quiet, suddenly every bit as sad as she was excited. He'd promised her a pleasurable goodbye with his words, with his eyes, with his hands already roving over her. The pleasure, she wanted. The goodbye, she did not.

"What are you thinking?" he asked, noticing her frown.

"Oh...I...nothing." *You will not fall apart over this.* She was determined to obey him, but even so, some tears squeezed from her eyes.

"Caitlyn."

"I know! I'm sorry."

He stood aside at the door and let her enter. She began at once to disrobe for him, trying not to let tears overwhelm her.

"It will be two weeks, Caitlyn. Perhaps less."

"I know," she said, her facade of control suddenly crumbling as she flew to his arms. "But...but...I'm so afraid. If you leave me...if you leave me alone..."

"You won't be alone. You no longer live alone in a cottage in the woods. You live in a fortified keep, protected by your husband's name and hundreds of soldiers."

"But you're leaving!" she sobbed into his neck.

"I'm leaving, but I'll return. You will be secure here until I come back."

"But what if you...what if you..."

"Don't come back?"

"Y...Y...Yes..." she cried. "Who will take care of me? The king? He hates me. He wants me dead."

"He doesn't want you dead, dearest."

"He does!"

"Hush," he said, trying to calm her. "Anyway, you won't go to the king. My father will take care of you should anything befall me. He'll find another husband for you if I don't return."

She gasped in horror at the very thought of it. "No. No! Your father?"

"I know you don't like him. But family is family. He won't leave you to the wolves. He'll find another match for you if you wish, or let you remain here as my widow. But honestly, Cait, I don't think I'll fall on a single journey to the Simpson holding and back. However, if I do, you must believe that you'll be provided for. My father and I have discussed it."

"You have?" She couldn't imagine it, that he would entrust her care into that man's hands, father or not.

"Yes. He's going to stay here until I return, so you must put your mind at ease."

The very idea of it made her cry even harder. How could he imagine that would put her mind at ease? But how could she beg him to send his own father away only based on her unreasonable fears? So he was an evil, bitter, malevolent old man. As long as he left her alone, she would be fine. She was surrounded by guards, by Henna, by townspeople who loved her. She would just stay in her room until Duncan returned.

She sniffed and signed, her course of action decided. She would simply have to hide away until Lord Douglas was gone. Duncan watched as she composed herself, wiping away her tears.

"Better now?"

She nodded, leaning close to him. "It's only because I love you so very much."

"I know," he said, drawing her back into his arms. "I love you too. I'll miss retiring to this room with you every night. And when I return..."

* * * * *

Oh, when he returned...

He would give her a send off tonight, but it would be nothing like the welcome he'd give her on his return. He looked down at her lovely breasts, heaving softly with her sobs. He cupped each one in his hand. Were they growing fuller? Duncan regarded them with a subtle narrowing of his eyes. His hands slid down to her hips, to her waist, and his fingers explored her there, encircled her as if seeing her anew. He sighed and cupped her chin in his hands.

"We will simply have to survive this short parting, Caitlyn."

"Yes sir."

"But before I go, dearest..." Light pressure had her sinking to her knees. Duncan fisted his cock and guided it to her lips. He closed his eyes, giving himself up to the warm, wet sensation of

Chapter Twelve

her eager mouth. He cupped the back of her head, drawing her closer, thrusting deeply in her throat. She gagged a little and worked to regain control, swallowing his length as he let his mind drift. But it returned again and again to this:

His beloved wife was with child.

There was only the slightest change. A darkening of her nipples, a subtle change in the size of her breasts, but he could see it. To his knowledge, her courses had not come on her as normal. Did she know? Did she even suspect?

He would let her discover it herself. He wouldn't tell her. To be truthful, he wasn't one hundred percent sure. He was only sure that her body was changing, and no one knew her body more intimately than he. Henna would know. She probably already knew. Duncan thought his innocent wife would be the last to realize her condition, and that only when her belly got too large to let her kneel down in position for him.

He pulled away from her and lifted her to the bed, spreading her legs wide and thrusting inside so that she gasped from the sudden adjustment of being filled by him. Her eyes closed with desire.

"Does that feel good, Cait?"

"Oh, yes. Yes!"

He took her hands in his and pinned them over her head. "Spread your legs for me. Spread them wider," he insisted, until her legs were splayed wide open and he could take her as deeply as he wished. He rode her hard. Her newly expansive breasts bounced with each thrust, and she tossed her head and grew wild from the sensation of him taking her so masterfully. It was as if he wanted to burn himself upon her since he wouldn't be able to be with her for some time. He let himself feel everything about her that he loved; her tightness, her warmth, her sighs against his ear, the heaving of her breasts beneath him as she orgasmed with breathless gasps.

He came inside her womb for the first time ever without anxiety. The thing was done. She was already with child. Well, he would still lie with her. It was impossible not to, and as soon as he returned, he would lie with her again. He would lie with her until her belly made it impossible. Even then, he thought he would still find a way.

But not tonight. He had to let her sleep because he intended to leave well before dawn. He intended to leave before she awakened. It would be too difficult to endure that tearful goodbye. He didn't want to see the fear that overwhelmed her. He knew she would be perfectly all right, and he would too, but she would fear the worst. It was more merciful to leave in the night. She would be angry, perhaps, because he had promised he would not leave her without saying goodbye.

So when she was fast asleep, when her breath came slow and steadily in the dark hours of the morning, he leaned close to her ear and whispered, "Good bye."

He rose and found Henna in the kitchen preparing a pre-dawn breakfast for the men. She knew him well enough to know by the look on his face what he'd come to tell her. She smiled.

"You'll see, Duncan. You'll have a fine son or daughter come summer. You'll see how silly you were to put this off."

"You knew already."

"Aye," she laughed, "but then, I know a woman's ways inside and out. I know how they change when they're carrying a bairn."

"Watch out for her, Henna. She doesn't know. Perhaps you shouldn't enlighten her until I return. She's already so nervous that something will happen to me."

"She'll miss her husband, yes. She's always had a singular attachment to you. I think it's sweet, how she dotes on ya. She hasn't known much security in her life."

Duncan sighed. "It's just a bit of business with the Simpson clan. I'll be back in a couple weeks. Just keep an eye on the little madwoman. Don't let her kill herself before I return."

Henna gasped. "Oh, to even say such a thing. She'll be perfectly fine. I'll keep her nice and busy with lots of projects. Now go on," urged the old woman. "Eat a good hot breakfast before ya go."

When Duncan rode out just before the light of dawn broke

Chapter Twelve

over the firth, he was trying to put his mind to the task at hand, the journey, but his mind kept returning to the thought of his sweet, slumbering wife all alone in his bed. He had the sudden mad thought of waking her and bringing her with him. He could place her before him in his lap to ride with him through the silent forests. She would have been an uncomplaining passenger, but it was impossible. Riding across Scotland, camping, surrounded by rough men. It was a fanciful idea. But it would have been nice to have her next to him to warm him all the way there and back.

Maybe if she wasn't pregnant he might have risked it, but it was much wiser in her condition to leave her safe at home. He put her out of his mind with great effort, and put his heels to his horse to catch up with his men in the dawn's light.

Chapter Thirteen

Cait walked the beach listlessly. A few days had passed but it still smarted to remember he had left her without saying goodbye. She sat on a rock near the water and dug her toes into the sand. He claimed he loved her, but he had a strange way of showing it. She drew shapes and squiggles in the damp earth, letting the waves roll up and wash them away.

She wouldn't write words. No. Ever since that day when Duncan learned she could read, everything had gone terribly wrong. She stabbed at the sand with the piece of driftwood, then looked back over her shoulder at Mitchum who stood at the mouth of the pathway to the beach. Mitchum didn't know she could read or write, nor did he care. She was so awfully lonely. She wished Mitchum would talk to her, keep her company, but none of them would. They only stalked along beside her, silent and attentive, looking around as if at any moment some mortal threat might present itself.

She considered walking back into town to gossip with the women, but it seemed they always held their tongues when she showed up. It was terribly uncomfortable. She wanted to listen in to their immoderate, girlish talk, to learn how other women pleased their husbands, but they always fell silent when she listened, and she simply wasn't in the mood today to play with the children.

She looked again at Mitchum, as if he might, against all hope, actually give her an idea of something to do. But he was looking past her, suddenly alert. She turned to find Lord Douglas only a few steps away. She leapt to her feet, and Mitchum began to walk towards them. How had he come to the beach without her or Mitchum noticing? The earl held up his hand.

"Come no closer, boy. I'll talk to my daughter-in-law in private. She'll come to no harm."

Mitchum took another step.

"Mind your place," said Douglas to Mitchum, and this time his voice was a warning. Mitchum stood where he was and didn't retreat.

Cait twisted her hands in the skirts of her gown.

"You have no curtsy for me, Princess?" Douglas asked, his eyes boring into her.

She made the smallest reverence possible. She had avoided the older earl thus far, but now, on this remote beach, she felt terribly imperiled. She snuck a look at Mitchum, who continued to watch as the earl drew her away. Lord Douglas ignored her subtle resistance.

"Do you like your guard there, what is the boy's name?" he asked when they were alone.

"His name is Mitchum, and he's not a boy."

"He is a boy, don't fool yourself. Do you like him?"

She looked up at the earl in confusion. "Like him? He is my guard."

"How would you feel if he was to be lost? You would be sad, wouldn't you? Say, if he was to fall from that rock up there?"

Cait's stomach turned over as the earl pointed casually to the rock jutting from the head of the cliff overlooking the firth. She went there often, although her guards would never let her near the edge.

"Say, if he was to fall, an unfortunate accident. All your fault. How would you feel?"

Cait swallowed hard. "Awful. But we don't go near the edge—we never go near the edge of that rock—"

"Don't you?" he said blandly. He looked at her. "If I want him to fall, he will."

Her throat closed up, and she had trouble breathing. "What do you want?"

"I want you to find a way to make him go away."

"He won't. He won't leave me. Duncan says—Duncan orders—"

"Duncan is not here, and your puffed up guards will not listen to me. He's already glaring, so I'll make this short. You will find a way to steal away from your guard tomorrow, and you will meet me at the abandoned barn on the hill beyond the orchard after lunch. If you do not find a way, your guard will die." He said it so calmly the entire world took on an air of unreality to her. She felt confused, breathless, shaky with fear.

"Why?" she asked, her eyes filling with tears.

"If you show distress, you will make it worse. Do you value their lives so little? Collect yourself. You will not know why. You will only do as I say, or else."

Cait looked over at Mitchum, so staunch, so protective. She couldn't be the cause of danger to him. With terrible effort, she schooled her face to calm obedience. "I will do as you say. Just don't hurt him. Don't hurt any of them. Please."

"That, my dear, depends on you."

Duncan. She needed Duncan. When would he be back? What could she do on her own without him? Who could she confide in? No one. It was not safe. If any harm came to Mitchum, or Lonnie, or Desmond, any of them, she couldn't bear the guilt. She would meet the earl tomorrow and see what he wanted. When Duncan returned, he would take care of all of this, but for now, she had no choice but to obey.

"What do you want?" she asked Lord Douglas again.

Chapter Thirteen

"You will learn that soon enough. And lest you think of telling anyone else about what we've discussed—"

"I won't," she interrupted before he could make any more threats. "May I go? It is nearly time for dinner."

Lord Douglas turned away and began to walk down the beach. Cait collected herself. She didn't know how she managed. She only knew she couldn't let Mitchum think anything was amiss. She walked over to him and forced a smile in the face of his obvious concern.

"What a nasty old man," she murmured. "It's getting late. Let's return to the keep."

* * * * *

All night Cait tried to think of a plausible excuse to get herself alone to the barn. She could simply steal away, but that would raise a terrible alarm, and would certainly infuriate the earl into possible retaliation. She would have to lie, but she was terrible at lying. She had no choice. She had to try.

The next day Henry was her guard, which was serendipitous. Of all of them, he was the least likely to question her. He usually barely attended her, and he had only been her guard a few weeks. She told him she was working on a surprise in the barn for her husband, that she wanted to complete it in secret before he arrived home. Henry seemed content enough with her excuse and allowed her to steal into the barn while he waited a distance away.

She pushed open the door, hoping against hope the earl wouldn't be there, but he was. He barred the door behind her as she backed across the barn. It was dark inside and dusty, a faint smell of animal still lingering in the air. Light filtered through some holes in the eaves. She shivered. It was terribly cold.

"Henry is here, but he's waiting a distance away. I told him I was coming here to work on a surprise." She watched him nervously. He just stared at her. Somehow it gave her comfort to keep talking, although she got the feeling he didn't care what she said. "For Duncan. A surprise for Duncan."

"Ah, a good plan," he said. "So you can come here every day without arousing suspicion."

"I'd rather not. I'd rather you just tell me what you want and get this over with. I don't enjoy all this secrecy. Duncan won't like it when he returns."

"Duncan will never learn anything of it," the earl said sharply. "I'm afraid that secrecy will continue to be required. Take your clothes off."

Cait's eyes widened. "I most certainly will not!"

"You will do what I ask, Princess, or someone you care for very much will be harmed."

Her eyes narrowed and she pretended a courage she did not feel. "You are a horrible man. I won't take my clothes off. Duncan forbade me to ever take my clothes off for another man—"

"Or he would punish you?" The earl's laughter was soft but terrible. "I warrant you have never felt a punishment like the one I've been reserving for you, dearest daughter-in-law. Now take your clothes off immediately, or I will do it myself."

* * * * *

Lord Douglas watched her pick at her food. He had stripped her of her dignity, her self-esteem, her belief in a safe, predictable world...and now her appetite as well. It pleased him. He liked the changes he'd seen in her. The deadening of her eyes, the stilted way she walked, the trembling in her hands. It was the way he'd always wished to see her. It had been an enjoyable week.

Soon, he would have to stop. There would have to be time for the marks to fade before Duncan returned from the Simpson keep. His entire plan had played out without a hitch. He didn't want to ruin it with something so simple as unhealed bruises and cuts. Tomorrow he would assault her for the last time. For now. Until Duncan left again. This lovely arrangement could go on for

Chapter Thirteen

years, as long as she had loved ones to threaten. As long as she valued the lives of her friends.

Everything had gone perfectly. The morose change in her demeanor was assumed to be a wife pining for her absent husband. No one suspected what went on up in the barn on the hill every afternoon. No one noticed him stealing in before she arrived or stealing away some time after she'd gone. Her guards believed she cried for *him* there, Duncan, because she missed him. Douglas chuckled to himself under his breath. No doubt the little whore did miss him when she was in that barn, for it was his absence that gave Douglas the opportunity he'd craved. He'd made good use of every moment with her. He'd abused the little slut in every way he knew.

The first day she'd been defiant. He'd had to wrestle her clothes off and shove her to the floor, cut off her breath until she complied, until she saw that *no* was not an option. He knew just how to do it without leaving marks. How to exert just enough pressure to immobilize a resisting woman, just enough to let them understand the threat that was at hand. After that she'd been still and let him have his way with her. And he had. Oh, he had.

He shifted, growing hard just thinking about it. His son obviously had his father's blood, for she was no stranger to the perverse ways he took her. That had disappointed him. He had wanted to make her quake and cry in shamed outrage. He had had to be rougher, more brutal to get the reactions he craved. When he'd slaked his lust, then he beat her. For that, he had to gag her first. She did try to be quiet. She didn't want her guards to be alerted to what was happening any more than he. But he wasn't willing to beat her any less brutally, so he resorted to a gag, a dirty piece of cloth he shoved in her mouth and tied with a leather belt around her head. He bound her hands too. He had to. He bound her completely when he wanted to mark her well. Sometimes he left her unbound for the fun of it, so he could stalk her around the barn with his lash. It was so thrilling to see the pleading, terrified eyes she turned on him. He never blindfolded her. No. He loved to see her eyes. It usually worked him up so much, beating her, that he was ready to use her again.

And he loved to see her now, sitting beside him at the table, every fiber of her being desperate to run away, to shrink away from him in horror. But she couldn't. *She couldn't.* It was too perfect. He would miss their afternoons. Tomorrow, he would have to beat her soundly enough to hold him over until next time. But he could still use her mouth, her ass, her cunt. He would. That would leave no telltale marks, not if he was careful. He could even beat her, if he was careful not to mark her. Oh, hell, in that case, what was the point? Why bother if he couldn't mark her, make her bleed? He wouldn't beat her. Next time. Next time.

No, he couldn't have Duncan discovering things. If his son ever learned what he'd done to his wife, he would kill him, cut him down in cold blood. Tomorrow was the absolute last day he could risk it. Tomorrow, he'd beat her well.

* * * * *

The gag impeded her breathing. She tried to calm herself, but the world spun before her eyes. She couldn't die. She musn't die, or she'd never see Duncan again. She needed him so desperately. She thought of him at times like these, when the pain was too much. The beating was too brutal...she was going to pass out. She wished she would. At least then she wouldn't feel it. But she never passed out. She was certain he knew exactly how far he could push her so she didn't reach that relief.

Breathe, breathe. Draw a breath in. Don't think about the bile rising in your throat. If she vomited she would choke. It had happened before. She just had to breathe and let her mind go away. *Duncan, Duncan, Duncan, Duncan.* Every time she thought of him tears came to her eyes. How would she survive? She had to survive it. She had to survive until he came home.

But then what? Douglas told her what would happen if she told him, poured threats in her ear, threats too vile to bear repeating, threats against Henna, her guards, even the children in town. She wished that she didn't believe him, but she did. She knew he was capable of murder, torture, any of those things. No one could do the things he'd done to her, say the things he'd said to her if they weren't depraved enough to take an innocent life.

He would take her life. He would. If he kept on beating her, whipping her, she would die. *Breathe, breathe, breathe.* Long slow breaths through the gag. She had to survive.

Finally he dropped the whip. She stayed curled up in the corner where she'd crawled just to lean against the wall, just to lean her forehead against the cool dirt there. He yanked her by the ankle, pulling her on her belly back into the center, holding her hips roughly to thrust inside. He used her bottom. He preferred it. She was so limp from the beating it barely hurt. Or maybe she was just so numb she couldn't feel his invasion. Either way, she was grateful the beating was done.

"You'll remember that for a while, my sweet, won't you?" he hissed in her ear as he defiled her. "You'll remember it until the next time I can get you alone. And believe me, there will be a next time."

She moaned behind the gag. She didn't want to. It always made him use her even more brutally, but the idea of a next time, it was impossible to bear. *Duncan, Duncan. Help me.* He couldn't help her. She couldn't risk telling him. He might keep her safe from Douglas, but he couldn't keep every innocent safe, every man, woman, child in the town. She couldn't bear to be the cause of anyone's death.

"I won't beat you again," he said when he'd finished and pulled away from her. He removed the foul gag. "You'll need time to heal before your husband returns."

Before your husband returns...before your husband returns. Duncan would return soon. He had to return.

"But I'll still use you, you dirty, wretched slut, since that won't leave marks. You'll report here just as you have been until the day your husband rides back into the courtyard. Now put your clothes on and get out of my sight."

Cait crawled to the door to put on her gown. She prayed the blood wouldn't stain her shift so much that she couldn't hide it from Henna. She'd destroyed three of them already, ripped them to shreds and buried them beyond the garden so there would be no questions to answer about the blood. She wished she could crawl into the ground herself. She was so tired. So tired.

He pulled her roughly to her feet when she'd dressed and kissed her on the mouth. "Smile, Caitlyn. Pretend you're happy," he said. "Or else."

She pushed open the door shakily. She took a deep breath, another. The outside air was bracing. It was getting colder. She could blame her breathlessness and shuddery shaking very easily on the chill. Desmond jumped up from the tree he leaned against when he saw her. She managed a tired smile.

"Hello, Desmond."

"How does your work come? What are you making for Lord Duncan?"

She looked at the ground, blinking, trying to think up a lie. "I...whatever I was working on...my surprise...I was trying to make him something, but I failed. I was trying to build...I was..." She grew silent. She was so tired. "I miss him so much."

She would fall to pieces if Desmond kept looking at her that way. He knew, he knew. He suspected.

"Are you unwell, lady? Is there anything I can do for you?"

She had to smile. She had to reassure him. *Not you, Desmond. He couldn't kill you.* "I'm fine, I'm only missing my husband."

"He'll be returning soon. He said it would be just a couple of weeks. He'll be home soon, you'll see."

"I hope so." But it couldn't be too soon. She was going to need time to heal. She couldn't even ask Henna for salve or medicine to help the healing. She had to sneak down and bathe as quickly as possible when Henna was busy at the other end of the keep and she could be sure of no one else attending her.

Soon, he would be home. Soon...

He had to come soon, or she'd throw herself from the rock herself.

Chapter Fourteen

Henna made her way down the corridor, chewing her lip. Something wasn't right. Something was amiss, she knew it for sure.

The lady was miserable. Yes, she was breeding, and yes, missing her husband too, but her grief was so deep, so all-encompassing. It wasn't natural for a lass to fall into such a spell. Henna assured her every day that the earl would return soon, that she wouldn't be missing him too much more, and then she'd lift herself out of her gloom with such false happiness that she seemed a different person altogether. Forced smiles, inane talk, an unnatural brightness in her eyes that made Henna wonder if she still possessed her wits.

Henna shook her head, looking down at the tray she carried. Try as she might, she could barely get the lass to eat. She tried every delicacy she knew to tempt the lady's appetite. At night, Cait sat pale and still at the table and looked positively green. Pregnancy, bah. It was a burden for women. Made 'em sick, made 'em strange and emotional-like. Well, Henna thought it was time to let her in on the secret. That, at least, would lift her spirits until Duncan returned.

She knocked softly and let herself in to find Cait already dressed and sitting on the edge of the bed. Again she forced one of those strained, false smiles.

"Good morning, Henna."

"Good morning, lass. How are ya doing? Perhaps this might be the day..."

"I hope so," she murmured without much conviction.

"I've brought you a tray. I want you to eat it. And mama Henna wants to have a talk with ya, if you don't mind."

Cait looked suddenly uneasy.

"A talk about what?"

"A talk about that wee little lad or lass that you're carrying now, love." Henna beamed and waited for Cait's reaction. But to Henna's surprise, instead of excitement, a look of consternation washed over her face.

"I don't...Are you sure...What...How do you know?"

"Have your courses come lately, when they should?"

"No. They haven't come this month. But perhaps it is only...some other reason..."

"And ye've been queasy and emotional. I can see you don't want to eat, and your moods, beggin' your pardon, they've been rather...unusual. It's clear to me you're carrying a babe. Won't Duncan be so happy to hear it? He's going to be a father, and you a momma at last, just as you wished."

Well, thought Henna as the silence stretched out, if the girl didn't look on the verge of tears!

"There now, don't you worry about nothing," Henna soothed. "Some women have trouble birthing babies, but you won't be one of those women. You mark my words."

"Oh, I know," said Cait, opening her hand on her middle. "I'm just...don't mind me. I just...don't know what to think. I didn't expect this. I didn't even think about this happening..." She closed her mouth and shut her eyes tightly. "Anyway, I think I shall rest."

"You'll eat first, lass. You must eat. You must feed the babe as well as yourself."

"Yes, I'll eat. When I wake up, perhaps. I promise I will."

Henna stood reluctantly, her eyes narrowed in suspicion. "Okay, then. I'll leave ya to rest."

She went back out into the corridor. No, that wasn't how she'd expected it to go at all. Something wasn't right. Something was amiss. She felt it in her bones. She knew it in her heart.

* * * * *

Cait lay back on the bed, appalled beyond belief. She had thought the beatings were the worst part, the pain and fear, the ever present threat, but no. No, this was the worst part. Beyond all things on earth, this was the worst.

She was carrying a child at long last, and it wasn't her husband's. It wasn't half-Cait, half-Duncan at all. It was half Cait and half *Devil*, the true Devil, the abominable, beastly old earl. How could it happen? How could her husband love her, seed her for so many months, and only now, in the last two weeks of violence and rape at the earl's hands, had seed finally taken root? How could it be? She wanted to cry bitter tears. It was so unfair, so against reason she couldn't get past the disbelief to give her grief voice.

She lay still, staring off into nothingness. What would she do? It would have to be kept secret. She would have to let Duncan believe he'd fathered it. But she...she would always know. She would have to live this lie, Lord Douglas's lies and secrets forever, even after the horrible old man ceased to live. Perhaps he would outlive her. Perhaps she would die bearing his child. It would satisfy him greatly to cause her death. How could she love such a baby, a baby begotten in misery? A bastard, she thought suddenly, just like her, just like Duncan. *A bastard for a bastard,* her father had scoffed once. *They will understand each other, will they not?*

No, she couldn't hate the baby, she wouldn't. It was not the baby's fault, and she couldn't let the child grow up alone and unwanted as she'd been. But the world, Cait realized now, was a horrid, awful place, a place she didn't want, a place she'd never belonged, a place she never would belong. She could no longer believe that life would bring anything but pain and grief.

She sat up at long last and checked beneath her garments. The welts and scabbed marks were still there. It had been over two weeks. He might return now, any moment, and he would want to see her in his bedroom. He would expect her to disrobe for him and make love with him as if nothing was amiss, as if she wasn't pregnant with the old earl's child and covered all over in the marks of his violence and hate. She thought suddenly, against all reason, that she didn't want Duncan to come.

She had thought, when he arrived, she would be safe at least a little while, that her mind would be at peace at least for a time. Now her peace was gone forever. How could she keep secrets from him? He would look at her and know. What if he found out? What would he do? Lord Douglas would find a way to blame her. It was too terrible a thought. She must hide it all, the baby, the marks, the secrets and lies.

At last, defeated, she slept and dreamed of horrible, nightmarish things.

* * * * *

Duncan rode ahead of the men. He was so close to home, it was impossible not to put his heels to his horse and run the rest of the way. He was so close, so close to his wife. He couldn't wait to get his hands on her.

He thought he would kill her from the weight of his unsatisfied desire. It would take hours and hours of using her to take the edge off the craving that drove him to her now, hard and fast and wild through the woods. But he would have to be gentle, tender, let her rest when he exhausted her...she was with child now, he remembered.

Even so, he would exhaust her with sheer pleasure, the lucky woman. He wouldn't leave her alone until they'd both been to heaven and back. And then...then he'd get an accounting of all her mischief. He laughed softly to himself. Then the fun would really begin.

He stopped to bathe in the lake on the rise, then continued down to the keep, throwing his reins to the stable boy when he arrived at the courtyard.

"The other men arrive soon," he said. He greeted those who greeted him, but his mind was on the one he sought. Henna bustled over, embracing him.

"Welcome home, my lord. How are the Simpsons?"

"Thank you, Henna. They are better now, better than when we first set upon them. Where is Caitlyn?" He frowned as he saw the concern in her eyes.

"What? What is it? The baby?"

"No—"

"What? Is she ill?"

"No, no. Calm yourself. It only seems that pregnancy does not agree with her much. She has been...strange."

"Strange?" Duncan looked around the hall. "Where is she?"

"Above stairs. Sleeping."

"Something's wrong. You're just not telling me." He headed for the stairs. "I knew, I knew I never should have—"

"Now, Duncan." Henna stepped in front of him. "You'll not begin already with this worry and agitation. She will be pregnant for many more months, and she will need you to be steadfast."

"Edana said she was in danger, she was in peril—perhaps this is what she meant! Perhaps she's ill—"

"I put no belief in her threats, and neither should you! The girl is fine, just breeding, and all that goes along with that, and you, of all people, must remain calm. If you wish to go to her, you must calm yourself first. I'll not allow it otherwise!"

Duncan took a deep breath and then laughed softly, composing himself, looking down at the frowning matron before him. She was half his height and portly as a fir bush, but he had no doubt she could prevent him passage if she wished.

"I'm calm, Henna," he said. "Calm and eager to see my wife. Let me pass and greet her before the other men arrive and I'm swept up in work."

"She is in her room," said Henna. "Kindly remember she is tired, and hasn't been eating well."

Tired? She may be tired and weak as a kitten, but he would still sink inside her before the hour was through. He scaled the stairs and walked quickly down the corridor. He stopped and knocked on the door before he opened it.

His wife. She was asleep, curled up under the covers. Ah, to see her pale, lovely skin, to feel her beautiful curves. He crossed the room to climb in beside her and pull her close.

"It is nearly noon, wife," he teased, "yet you laze here in bed."

She awakened with a start as his arms came around her. She had far too many clothes on. He began to pull up her skirt.

"No!" she gasped, pulling away from him.

He froze. She burst into tears, reaching out for him.

"Duncan, I'm sorry." She clung to him, sobbing bitterly, practically strangling him, but the next moment pulled away from him again. Henna was right. Pregnancy had addled her mind. He tried to soothe her.

"I want you, Cait. I want to hold you. I've been missing you. I've been away from you too long. Undress for me."

"But...but...it's daylight."

"I don't care."

He stood and began to take his clothes off. She rose unsteadily from the bed and backed away.

"I...I cannot lie with you, my lord," she stammered.

Duncan smiled. "Is there something you want to tell me, dearest? Some news? I promise you, it won't keep me from your bed. Not now, not in your ninth month."

Caitlyn shook her head, anxious and pale. Her eyes looked positively wild. He grew still, half undressed. Something was wrong. Henna was right. She wasn't well.

"What is it, Cait? What are you afraid of?"

"I'm just...I...I haven't seen you in so long..."

"Even so, we are not strangers to one another. You know very well what I want, and that you will enjoy it. Come, you haven't even given me a kiss."

He held out his arms, but she didn't come. *She didn't come.*

"It's only...it is only that I didn't bathe last eve. My gown is...dirty...my underthings...I must go bathe," she said in a rush, darting out the door.

And he would have caught her, he would have stopped her if he wasn't so shocked to see her lie, bold and outright, to his face. *She lied to him.* But why? Why?

He dressed again and made his way after her to the kitchens. He nearly caught her at the door to the washroom, but then, against all reason, his wife shut and locked the door.

She was mad. She'd completely taken leave of her senses. All around him, the kitchen staff stopped their work and stared. He banged on the door nonetheless, blind to everyone but his strange, mad wife.

"Caitlyn, if I have to break this door down you'll regret it. Open it, now!"

Henna bustled in and scolded the open-mouthed staff back to work. She came to join Duncan at the door.

"She's locked me out," he said. "You're right. She's not well. Something's wrong with her."

Henna rattled the door. "Lass. Let me in."

"Caitlyn! Open this door right now or I'll redden your behind!"

"Hush!" scolded Henna. "You let her be. She's just—"

"Just what? Just running and hiding from her own husband? She looked at me and backed away as if I intended her harm!"

"She's breeding. She's addled. Just let me handle this!" She turned to the door and softened her tone into a motherly croon. "There now, lass, let mama Henna in. Let me in, and I'll help you wash your hair." *You go away,* she mouthed to Duncan under her breath.

He shook his head firmly and then, as both of them leaned on the door, the lock gave way. The door flew open and they saw Caitlyn huddled in the corner. She took one look at Duncan's scowl and Henna's puzzled stare and fainted dead away.

They both ran to her.

"Loosen her clothes," said Henna. "I'll tell them to bring some water for a warm bath."

The servants bustled in, filling the tub. Duncan wet a cool cloth and swabbed her pallid face.

"Henna, she's ill."

"She was not ill before. I didn't realize she was ailing so!"

Not just ailing. It was as if she'd lost her mind, thought Duncan. The woman who'd avoided him, stammered over her words, lied to him was not the Caitlyn he knew. As the servants filed out, he and Henna undressed her. She was still clearly with child, the changes subtle but noticable. But she was so pale and thin.

"Lift her into the tub," Henna told Duncan when Cait was fully undressed. "Carefully..." She followed behind and then with a horrified gasp, she cried, "No!"

Duncan spun with her in his arms. "What?"

"No, no, no!" Henna repeated again and again, her face drained of color. "Her back, her back! Oh, what evil—"

He sat and leaned her forward in his lap, taking in the sight of his wife's back and buttocks. His breath left him. He stared at the angry marks, disbelieving. He couldn't form the words he needed to say. He couldn't move, he couldn't do what he needed to do, which was murder whatever man had done this to his wife. Whatever man had defiled her, hurt her this way, he would tear him to pieces with his bare hands. He would torture him until he begged for death, and then he would give him death, agonizingly slow and painful. But first...first he would know his name.

Henna was already returning with armfuls of salves and ointments. "Hold her. Let me tend these...these...wounds before they fester." As she worked, fat tears rolled down her cheeks. "I didn't know. I didn't know, my lord. I still don't know, I swear. I have no idea where... what...how..."

Blood rushed in Duncan's veins, an angry whoosh and beat in his ears. "When I find out..."

"She comes to. Hush. Don't frighten her."

Cait shifted in his arms with a moan as Henna tended to her back. Somehow, he knew not how, he kept his temper and waited for her to wake before speaking to her quietly.

"Cait. I need to know right away what happened to you. I need to know who...beat you." He could barely say the words, it was so outrageous. He would viciously murder whoever did it. He would tear them limb from limb.

"Tell me," he prompted when she didn't answer.

"I...I...I fell from a tree—"

"Caitlyn—"

"In the orchard. I fell from the top. It was terrible—"

"Caitlyn, who? Who are you protecting? One of your guards? Which one? Give me the name."

"No!" she cried out, horrified. "No, it was not one of them. It was...I...I fell from a tree. I swear."

"I will bring your guards here," he said, "and I will torture them one by one until you tell me the truth." It was an awful thing to say, a trick he'd learned from his father. Threaten to harm those loved the most, to get your way. *His father. A trick he'd learned from his father.* His blood ran cold.

"I fell from a tree," she wailed. "No one harmed me. You must believe me!"

"What did he say? What did he tell you?" Duncan said, his heart thumping in his chest. "That he would kill someone if you told? My father did this to you."

"No, no, no!" she insisted hysterically. "I...it was no one...I fell from a tree!"

"My father did this. Tell me!" he ordered, suddenly enraged. "Tell me the truth!"

She sobbed. "I...I can't!"

He backed away from her and left her to Henna. He wanted to soothe her. He wanted to care for her, but his rage, his fury was too great. He needed revenge. He would kill his father. He strode to the courtyard to find the devil and his men already fled.

He called his men to arms. He would catch them on the way back to their castle. He wouldn't rest until revenge was his.

* * * * *

Lord Douglas and his men traveled west, not south. As soon as he'd seen Duncan ride into the courtyard, he'd readied his soldiers to go. He knew it was too soon. Stupid bitch. If she hadn't driven him on, driven him to beat her ever harder, long past the time he safely should have...

Stupid whore. This was all her fault.

Duncan wasn't nearly as stupid as his sluttish wife was. He would figure out in short order who had marked her gorgeous back and legs and ass. His son would fly to Southbrook to confront and accuse him, but he wouldn't be there.

No, he had a better plan, brilliant in its simplicity. They rode west a short distance from Inverness and waited for it to grow dark. He couldn't return to Southbrook, not until his son was dead or incapacitated, or until he got over his fawning affection for his wife, which probably wouldn't be anytime soon.

Until then, he would not be safe at his own holding, or anywhere near Inverness and Duncan's lands. But he knew a small, unremarked hideaway in the wild woods near Dunain. He would take his few men and go there and consider what to do. But not yet. He wouldn't go yet, not until he tried one last caper just for fun.

* * * * *

Cait lay awake in bed, unable to sleep. Her husband was gone. He had left her in a fury of anger and disgust. He knew. Of course he had known. She hadn't been able to hide it from him.

He would know everything, and he would revile her for it. He would pretend he didn't revile her, but he would. And what would Lord Douglas do now? His many threats battered around in her brain. If he hurt anyone, it would be all her fault. The men of the keep were scattered, and the entire house was at ends, only quieting now, finally, in the dark hours of the night.

She was so tired, so tired. Her mind spun wearily. The men were gone. She was left behind again. She was just as she would always be...unwanted and despised. She couldn't bear it. It was too sad.

She heard a soft, scratching knock at the door. She was too bereft to stir.

"Madam!" a voice whispered through the door. "I've come from your husband. I have a message for you."

Cait sat up, suddenly alert. He'd sent a message. She went to the door and cracked it slightly.

One of Duncan's men stood outside, although he was not familiar to her.

"My name is James. Your husband sent me to fetch you."

"Where is he? Where is my guard?"

"He's readying the horse for you, so we can get away quickly. Your husband wants to see you. He doesn't want you to be alone on this difficult night."

"Has he been to Lord Douglas's keep?"

"Not yet, lady. Come, we shouldn't waste time in talk. Your husband says he wants you to come."

Her husband wanted her. She wanted him too.

"Come quietly, lady," the guard cautioned. "The household sleeps."

The courtyard was empty, and he led her under cover of the shadows to a waiting horse. There was only one. But by the time she realized he wasn't who he said he was, it was far, far too late to scream.

Chapter Fifteen

Six weeks, Duncan thought miserably. It had been six weeks since he'd left her alone, gone running after a man he had yet to find, leaving her behind to be plucked right from under his fingertips. His father had his wife. He knew not where.

He only knew he was harming her, if she wasn't already dead.

He took another deep drink. Henna frowned from the door, and Connor sighed across the table. He didn't care. Let them all mutter and stare, and turn away from him in pity. He was not giving up. He would never give up. But he had to drink to sleep. He had to drink until his mind stopped working, until he could stop remembering the livid marks he'd seen, stop imagining how many more were on her now.

Cait. I'm so sorry. I'm so sorry. I can't even say...

It didn't matter how sorry he was, how much he regretted letting go of her. He should have held her. He shouldn't have let her go. But he'd left her, stormed off thinking only of his own bitter vengeance. He hadn't even taken the time to say goodbye.

He buried his head in his hands. *Goodbye. Goodbye.* More

and more, he feared he would never see her again. She could be anywhere. Douglas could have taken her out of Scotland, or tossed her to the bottom of the firth. No one knew better than he that his father was heartless. And he, for some reason, had left her with him. He'd been so wrapped up in his own thoughts, his own pleasure, his own needs and wants and duties. He hadn't even considered her fears and apprehensions. He had taken her for granted, thought her a silly, overemotional girl. He had left her with his *father*.

Now he had nothing at all.

He groaned under his breath. Connor shifted across from him.

"My lord. The hour grows late—"

He fell silent at the look Duncan gave when he lifted his head.

"Not drunk enough. Not yet." His head dropped again to the table.

Connor shifted as Henna called from the doorway, announcing a visitor. He nudged his lord.

"Duncan. Someone comes!"

At the tone in his friend's voice, Duncan rose unsteadily to his feet. He saw her in the doorway, long black curls and pale blue eyes.

Cait.

No, it wasn't Cait. Not Cait. Edana. At last.

"I've been waiting for you." He meant to sound angry, frustrated, furious, all the things that he felt as he waited for her. But he didn't. He sounded weak and forlorn. Hopeless. Defeated. "Where is she, Edana? Please tell me. Please tell me you know."

"I don't know."

"Is she alive?"

"She lives. I feel it. I see her. She's in Scotland. She isn't terribly far."

"My father took her. He...he...harmed her."

"I told you she was in danger," the priestess said. She looked so much like Cait, it seared him to his soul. He shook his head.

"I never thought...my own father...my own wife..." He looked at her reproachfully. "I've waited for you to come. What took you so long? I'm...losing hope. I've searched the woods every day. Dead winter comes, and she...she must come home. She is with child."

Edana sighed. "It was you I felt calling, not her. It is you who drew me here."

"But she is your daughter. Can't you go into a trance or something? Divine where she is? Isn't that within your powers?"

"Sometimes. My powers are a gift of the Goddess. Sometimes She gives the sight. Sometimes She does not."

Henna came forward with a tray of food and drink for the priestess, but she waved it away.

"No. I will fast. You will help me, woman. You are the healer here?"

Henna nodded.

"Come. Show me the highest, most open vantage point in the keep. I will meditate and fast until dawn. Tell your men to be ready. We will not find her by skulking about here."

* * * * *

Cait hunched over outside the cottage. She rocked slowly, trailing her fingers through the dirt, remembering him. She couldn't think of his name. It was too horribly painful to think it, to remember his hands, his warmth, his lips. His gentleness. She kept his name inside her heart, like a treasure, locked away.

Locked away, just as she was.

She'd tried to escape. So many times she'd started walking, started running directionless through the woods. She wasn't locked away behind any door, any iron bars or windows. She was locked behind a wilderness of endless, impenetrable woods. And so she waited, but everyday she hoped a little less.

Soon enough, she knew, the old earl would understand about the baby. She didn't know what he would do. She never knew what he would do, only that it would be wicked and violent and painful. It would be impossible to endure if he harmed the baby. Even though it wasn't Duncan's, she loved it all the same. It was the only thing that comforted her as the lonely weeks went by. As long as the baby was inside her, he couldn't harm it. Unless he killed her, which he threatened to do all the time. *When I grow tired of you, Princess, I'll throw you from the tower. So you had best not grow tiresome. You had best do as I say.*

And she did do everything he demanded of her. She learned that abject obeisance could sometimes stave off his ire. She groveled, she cowered, she begged and cringed and shrunk before him. When he demanded it, she bowed and served his men. More and more he passed her off to them, drowning himself in drink while they used her one after the other. He was growing tired of her. Perhaps the end would come soon.

She had no way of knowing, and thinking about it only troubled her already unquiet mind. She couldn't think as she used to. Her wits were going hazy. It was a blessing. She lived moment by moment, tried to live outside the atrocities he visited on her. And most of all, for her sanity, she didn't think of *him.*

Only once a day, at dusk, while the earl drank with his henchmen, she allowed herself to look up at the sky and think that, perhaps, he too looked up and thought of her. She thought hard, every night. *I'm here, Duncan. Wherever here is.*

Please come.

* * * * *

"Come!" shrilled Edana. "We are close. I can feel it."

For a week now, at dusk, she had led Duncan and his men deeper and deeper into the woods outside Dunain, through trees and brush so thick that the horses balked and progress was slow. But Edana pressed forward urgently, as if Caitlyn's voice herself was calling aloud.

"Stay together!" he barked to his men. He believed that Edana was leading them to Cait, but he also knew his father would not be alone. Duncan had brought an army one hundred strong to bring her home.

Edana paused, closing her eyes. The army of men fell silent

as the grave, so silent one could hear the whispering of the wind in the trees. Even the horses seemed to hold their breath, not shifting, not exhaling. For a long moment, she meditated, then opened her eyes and turned to the west.

"She is near." Duncan's hair stood on end as it always did when she spoke in that voice. "She is near. She lives. She waits. She calls to you," she finished in a whisper edged with tears.

He looked at the steadfast woman, her back straight, her chin jutting forward stubbornly even as he heard the tremor in her voice. He'd never even considered her own grief. Cait was her daughter, as well as his wife. Of course this must be difficult for her as well. He thought sometimes that Edana felt and saw things she didn't tell him. He saw her lips go white, saw her eyes close in pain, but he was too afraid to ask...

"Tonight?" he asked instead, his voice hopeful. "Tonight?" he asked again when she didn't respond.

"I don't know." She waited, shaking her head. "No, I've lost her. Tomorrow," she said with determination. "Tomorrow at dusk, we will search again."

Duncan's shoulders slumped in the fading twilight. Another day. It was excruciating when he, too, could feel they were near.

"She is west, you believe? Shall we go west?"

"The light is fading."

"I cannot wait," he said through gritted teeth. "God help me, I cannot wait. These nights, these days...I cannot bear them—"

"I hear her only at dusk!" snapped Edana. "I am doing all I can! I do not wish to wander around blind and end up further away! We wait until dusk tomorrow, to be sure of our direction!"

Duncan sighed and walked away from her. He would walk all night. They could stay where they were, but for himself, he would walk. He would walk until he tripped over the godforsaken hiding place where she was. He could hear the men dismounting, preparing to camp for the night. He turned around, then stood still as stone, looked and listened. There was no fire, no sound, no light that he could see, and yet he *knew*. She was so near. He could feel her, he could sense her. He could *smell* her in

Chapter Fifteen

the air.

He looked up at the darkening sky, then down at his feet. His eyes widened in astonishment and he fell to his knees.

His name was written there in the dirt, his own name in quickly scrawled letters.

DUNCAN

It was his name written in her hand. Her letters, right there. The message was hidden in the shadow of thick brush.

And beside his name, making his blood pound in his veins, an arrow pointed the way.

* * * * *

They uncovered the enclave just before dawn. It was only a small holding, a cottage, some outbuildings, the ruins of a keep. From outside, it looked sleepy and peaceful. A few of his father's men slept in the open air of the overgrown courtyard. No one kept watch. Edana led Duncan to a small storehouse behind the cottage. It was locked, but Duncan had it open with a silent swipe of his weapon. He motioned Edana to wait but she would not be deterred. They entered the small room together. It was dark, dank. Freezing.

She was there.

She stirred on the pallet on the ground, waking only slightly. She turned away, hunched in a miserable ball.

"She thinks you are him," whispered Edana.

Duncan crossed the small distance in a heartbeat and took her in his arms. She resisted with a soft sob.

"Cait, it is me. Caitlyn, my dearest..."

She turned to him, her eyes dull with disbelief. She reached out to touch him mournfully.

"It is a dream. A dream only..."

"It is no dream, Cait. I promise. It's me."

She reached to put her cool palm to his cheek, then pulled it away as if he burned her.

"It's you," she gasped, throwing her arms around his neck.

He embraced her, letting go when he felt her wince. Her clothes were ragged, dirty; her skin pale and bruised. The rank blanket she pulled around her was woefully inadequate and thin for the bitter cold. Her lovely black curls hung lank and tangled, but she was still the most beautiful sight he'd ever beheld in his life.

He beckoned Edana forward.

"Caitlyn, I swore to myself I would never, ever leave you again. But there is something I must take care of that no lady should be a party to. Stay here with Edana. Your mother. She will watch over you until I return."

Cait's fingers twisted in his vest. "I want to come with you."

"You cannot. It's not safe. I will not be long."

He untwisted her fingers gently and kissed them, and looked deep into her eyes. "You will be safe here until I return for you. And I swear to you, I will return."

Before he could fall to the pleading in her eyes, he turned and strode from the shed. He beckoned his men around him. Lord Douglas's men would soon be stirring.

"Put every one of these blackguards to the sword," Duncan said. "But leave my father to me."

* * * * *

Cait shivered violently. He was there, but now gone again. He had only been a dream after all. It was surely a dream, for now the strange woman who looked exactly like her was approaching as the morning half-light that filtered through the cracks in the wall. She remembered her from past dreams, in her woad dress with her long black hair. The Cait-woman was pulling off her cloak and wrapping it around her. For a dream, the cloak felt amazingly warm and real. But Duncan was gone, and she would soon awaken, and this strange older version of herself was whispering in her ear. Perhaps she had died. Could it be? She didn't remember dying. She must only be dreaming. But it had seemed so real. He had felt so real, she had let herself believe this time.

"It was no dream," the woman said. "You are awake. He will return."

Cait looked at her, shaking her head. She would not raise her hopes again, only to have them dashed.

"You may pinch me if you wish, and see if you hurt me," said the woman with a smile. "If it will make you believe."

Cait only looked at her. She would not talk to a specter. She would not interact with a dream. She was losing her mind, but she was not that far gone yet. The woman studied her, looking thoughtfully into her eyes.

"'Tis true, is it not? You favor me more than a little. Your father said as much."

"You knew my father?" she asked before she could stop herself. "My father is a king. He would help me. Can he help me, do you think?"

"Your husband is here. You need no help now. But yes, the king would have helped you if he had known you needed help. He is not so gifted as we are, to know when help is needed. Or perhaps he is only too preoccupied with worldly concerns."

"You know the king?"

Edana smiled again. "Child, I am your mother, as much as he is your sire. We know one another. There is no other way."

"You are my mother?" Cait was terribly confused. She had no mother.

"I am. I'm afraid I've been an absent, neglectful mother to you. I thought it was better that way, but perhaps I was wrong. You must forgive me if you can find it in your heart. I would like us to be friends."

Cait fell silent again, thinking, untangling. She was safe. It was not a dream. Duncan was returning soon. She could hear the shouts of Lord Douglas's men, hear the clanging metal and the violence outside.

"It will be all right," the woman assured her. "They will

prevail."

They would prevail. She had a mother. This woman was her mother. At last the tears came. Edana took her in her arms and rocked her gently.

"When will he return? When?" Cait sobbed.

"Hush now. Soon."

* * * * *

The raid was over in minutes. His father's men died violently, like the beasts they were. A few cowards scattered, outlawed, into the woods. Duncan's men found Lord Douglas passed out over his cup at the table. They trussed him hand and foot and brought him before their lord. Even in his dire position, the old earl sneered at him.

"Are you sure you want her back, Duncan? I believe you may find her changed. She is not quite so pure as I found her, but a great lot more obedient and demure."

Duncan didn't flinch, just kept cleaning the blood from his weapon. His men ranged around at an appropriate distance, ready to help if needed. But they knew this was a confrontation Duncan needed to settle on his own.

"Changed?" Duncan echoed quietly. "She is the same. The same sweet woman she was when her mother brought her to this world. I think it is you that has changed."

"Me? Yes, I have changed. I've become much more miserable since I met your harlot of a wife, whiling away my time here at this deserted keep with only her skinny, worthless body to pass the time—"

"I never knew you to love a woman," Duncan interrupted. "Too high and mighty, too manly to stoop so low. All that nonsense."

Lord Douglas laughed wildly. "I have never met a woman worthy of love."

"Until you met my wife."

"Disgusting, petty creatures, all of them. Vain and unconstant and only good for one thing."

"Good for one thing? I've heard that for a lifetime, but I don't think that's what you really believe. I think you destroy whatever is innocent and good because you are so vile and worthless in your own eyes and the eyes of everyone who knows you—"

"You are an idiot, Duncan," said Douglas, forcing a smile. "You will never understand."

"Did you rape my own mother, you blackhearted devil?"

"Perhaps I did. What difference does it make? She was only a woman, like all the other useless women on earth. Just one more sluttish female to beleaguer the male species—"

His voice fell silent as Duncan braced his sword a hair's breadth from his neck. "Not one more word."

"Will you kill your own father? You haven't the nerve. You've always been soft, too emotional and womanish for your own good. You call yourself a soldier, but you're no better than the weak, brainless slut who bore you."

"You will not compel me to kill you quickly, old man. I know what you're about. No. I think you will be made to suffer just as she did. A few cuts, a certain organ of yours mutilated beyond repair. Some blood to draw the wolves from the woods." He looked around thoughtfully, considering. "I'll have you staked to the front of the cottage. That would be best. I hope you survive for days, and I pray you die sensible with the teeth of wild animals at your throat." He lowered his sword, signaling his men. "But I cannot stay to enjoy your demise. I must take Cait and our babe where they will be safe."

"*Our* babe? The babe is mine, Duncan. She told me."

Duncan laughed, shaking his head. "Caitlyn is ignorant in these things. She always has been, and perhaps always will be. But I tell you, the babe is mine. And while it unfortunately has your blood as well, I hope Cait's goodness will finally overcome that taint."

He turned his back on his father. He'd seen enough of his evil face to last a lifetime. He would not have the murder of his father on his soul, devil though he was. But he would see that it happened just the same. He would leave it to his men and their own outraged fury, and take Caitlyn far away from here, and pray she could forgive him for the unspeakable evil he'd brought to her life.

"He is yours," he said to his men, who hovered impatiently to wreak revenge on behalf of their lady. "Take your time about it, and don't be too kind. As for me and my wife, we return to Inverness at once. It's possible his screams for mercy could disturb her," he added as an afterthought. "Wait just a while until we are away."

* * * * *

Cait leaned back against Duncan, listening to his steady heartbeat. His arms were wrapped tightly around her and his hands rested on her as he held to the reins. He seemed unwilling to let her stray even an inch from his body. When she shifted, his arms tightened to pull her closer again. It took until nightfall to reach the keep on horseback. Cait slept through most of the journey. At the keep she was handed over to Henna, who fussed and keened in her ear.

"Oh, child, how can you ever forgive me?" she wailed, wringing her hands.

Cait was so tired she barely heard her, but Henna's hands were gentle and soothing, and for that she was grateful. The women took her torn clothes and shoes and burned them at Duncan's command. They bathed her in warm, scented water for over an hour, washing her hair, tending her smarting cuts and bruises. Henna and Edana put warm scented salve on the worst ones and covered them with clean linen bandages. When she was nearly asleep, they laid her in bed. Duncan's bed. She was not too sleepy to realize that. He paced and hovered, coming in and out of her line of sight as the women examined her.

"The baby lives," Edana finally said. Duncan exhaled in relief. "You are four months along, Cait, if not more. It is not Douglas's child. This child was conceived of your husband long before that blackguard stole you away."

It is not Douglas's child. *It is not Douglas's child.* Cait smiled. It was their child, half-Duncan, half-Cait, just as it should be. She wanted to tell them how happy she was, how pleased, but the only thing that came out of her mouth was, "I'm tired."

"You must eat," said Henna. "Do not sleep until you've had a good meal. Think of the babe."

Her eyes closed as she felt Duncan's arms come around her. She didn't need food or drink. She just needed him.

* * * * *

Duncan looked down at his wife's exhausted features. He could feel her body relax into sleep.

"Poor creature," said Henna. "Poor, poor creature. She'll never forgive me. She won't. She shouldn't!"

"She will," said Duncan. "She would never blame you. Knowing Cait, she blames herself for all of this." He brushed her damp hair back from her cheek. "I am the one to blame. This was all my fault."

"I will stay," said Edana suddenly. "I will stay some time and help her heal."

Henna and Duncan exchanged glances. "There is no need, Edana. Henna can tend to her."

"I mean her mind, not her body. Her mind is unwell. As is yours," she added, looking at Duncan. "I will stay until I know my daughter is better."

Duncan frowned. "As you wish."

"I will not steal her away from you, if that's what your dark looks are all about. She possesses more power than I suspected, but the life of a priestess is not for her."

"Power?" Duncan echoed. But looking down at her in his arms, he knew exactly of what she spoke.

Chapter Sixteen

Duncan jerked awake to the sound of Cait's screams, and gathered her up for the second time that night.

Edana had been right. Her mind was troubled, even though she tried to pretend she was perfectly fine. Little by little, after sleep and healing, she had risen from her bed and gone about her life with an endearingly plucky determination to "forget about that horrible man." By day she did many of the same things she used to. She roamed the town, tended the gardens, even walked on the beach. But at night, it was clear to Duncan that she still suffered. At night, when she slept, Lord Douglas came to her in her dreams.

"Shh, shh.." he crooned, waiting patiently for her to stop struggling, to realize it was him holding her and not his father. As soon as she did, she curled against him with that familiar relieved sigh.

God, he hated that she hurt.

Edana had left recently, promising to return at high summer for the birth of the babe. He had to admit she had been very wise

Chapter Sixteen

at healing. She had spent long hours talking and bonding with her daughter. Edana was responsible for the positive changes he saw in Cait, the new confidence and strength of will. He knew Edana was no small part of the reason Cait seemed so calm and adjusted after her ordeal, at least during the day. It was certainly no doing of his. He had been so agitated and cowed by the damage done to her he had avoided her, giving her over to Edana every morning in relief. Henna slunk about as guiltily as Duncan. But Cait, she was so strong. She took it all in with clear eyes and an innocent heart and truly seemed content to let it all go.

Until she slept.

Their nights, which used to be a dream world of intimacy and pleasure, were transformed into trials for them both. He could not even think about reaching out to her in lust, although he burned beside her as he always had. She awoke with screams, and he awoke with an intense arousal that he did his best to hide. Her body tempted him mercilessly. Her curves rounded out as she regained her appetite and the sickness of her early pregnancy eased away. There was a pronounced curve to her belly now that he longed to kiss and caress, and her breasts...they would fill his hands if he could only touch them as he craved.

But he couldn't. He couldn't touch her in any way that a man touched his woman. He couldn't bear to touch her and feel her pull away from him in disgust, or even worse, fear. So they went on much as they had in the beginning, him avoiding her as much as possible except in the night, when they lay miserable and uneasy next to one another in bed.

He had wanted to ask Edana her advice, but in the end he couldn't do it. He couldn't admit that he even desired to use his wife, much less ask her advice on how best to go about it. No, he couldn't. For now, he would have to go without. He didn't deserve her anyway.

And she was pregnant, he reminded himself. The only thing that was important right now was Cait's well-being, her health and the babe's. If and when his wife ever wanted him again in that capacity, she could make the overtures herself.

Cait and the Devil

Cait walked heavily up the hill to the orchard. It seemed an age ago that she'd snuck here to get his attention and ended up turned over his lap. Silly, childish games, she thought, from when she was still young and innocent. She was not innocent now. She never would be again.

Duncan knew it. He didn't even want her anymore, now that she was so used. He deigned to even touch her. In bed, he held himself away even though he soothed her fears. He probably wished she'd move back into her old room and not plague him with nightmares all night long, but she couldn't sleep so far away from him. She would put up with his carefully cultivated distance, with his restrained touch, if only to sleep there next to him and know he was only an arm's length away.

As she drew nearer to her favored tree, she looked over at Desmond. He bit his lip and avoided her gaze. Even her guards tiptoed around her now. Before, he would have warned her that her husband didn't like her climbing up in trees. Now he just frowned and kept his silence. Their behavior—Duncan's, Henna's, her guards'—did nothing more than remind her what had happened, again and again. She scowled, looking away from him.

Only Edana treated her like a real person since her return, and she was gone now. *Edana.* She couldn't call her *mother*, and she didn't think Edana wanted her to. She was not much like a mother anyway, more like a wise friend. She had made Cait feel for the first time that she was not worthless, that she was not ugly and unwanted. She looked like Edana, and Edana was truly beautiful, so she must be too, at least a little. And Edana, her mother, was a great priestess. At least some of that intelligence and poise must run in her veins.

"Don't forget that you have great power of your own, my love," Edana had told her.

"Power? What kind of power?" Cait asked doubtfully.

"The power of a warm and innocent heart. I am not innocent, nor could I ever be, but you have the ability to look at the world through clear eyes, unfiltered by guise and pride and scheming. It is a gift, my dear, and not many have it."

"It doesn't do me much good, honestly."

Edana had laughed at that, but it was true. She looked through her clear eyes at her husband, but he avoided her gaze. She looked at Henna and she skittered away. She looked at her guards and they averted their eyes. No one wanted to see what was there.

So be it. She would have a baby to care for soon. Her baby would love to stare into her eyes and smile and tug at her hair as she'd seen the other babies do to their mamas. Her baby wouldn't know or care what Lord Douglas had done to her.

She reached the tree she loved most, with all the good broad branches for climbing. She could sit low and still feel she was hidden in a secret place, or she could climb high and be safely supported by the strong boughs. She felt like really climbing high today.

Desmond cleared his throat as she hoisted herself up into the cradle of the twisted trunk to climb onto the first branch.

"Lady, you should not climb in your...your condition."

"I can climb just fine."

"Your husband will not like it."

"Won't he? Then he can come and get me down." *If he cares about me, let him come.*

She didn't climb as high as she might have, because Desmond was eyeing her, coughing and frowning and scowling the higher she climbed. She made herself comfortable in a seat between two large boughs and looked around. She could see the keep, the grounds, everything from this vantage point. Spring had not quite arrived, no leaves yet bloomed.

"Can you see me, Desmond, or do the branches hide me?"

"I can see you fine, ma'am." He frowned up at her, muttering something about how it would be *his* neck if she fell, just loudly enough for her to hear. Well, she would not fall. She was an expert climber. She had been her entire life. She'd been raised in a forest, she wanted to remind him, but she kept her silence.

She sat for several minutes looking around, wishing there were apples to pick, before she noticed Duncan start across the field. She probably could have eaten a dozen apples. Her appetite lately was unmatched. But there weren't any now, nor any green leaves to hide herself, so she just waited and watched through the branches as her husband came near.

He was so comely, so handsome. Even the way he walked affected her. She remembered him crossing the bedroom to her with that walk. Intent, strong, focused. He looked a lot like Lord Douglas, but at the same time, nothing like him, because his eyes were so kind. Even now, when his face looked angry, his eyes were gentle, not cold and horrid like his father's.

When he arrived, he dismissed Desmond with some short words and crossed his arms, glaring up from under the tree.

"Come down, Caitlyn. Immediately."

She should obey, shouldn't she? She looked down at him, at his broad shoulders, his stern expression.

"I don't really want to. I like it up here."

"That may be so, but if you do not climb down from that tree this instant I will spank your disobedient bottom, six months pregnant or not."

She shifted on the hard branch. He hadn't touched her like that in weeks. He hadn't spanked her or caressed her or given her his seed. She swung her legs and picked at some bark.

"If you want me, I suppose you can climb up here and haul me down."

He frowned so darkly that Cait had the sudden urge to giggle. Laughing at him now would probably be going too far. Perhaps she had already gone too far, but she didn't care.

"Caitlyn, do not test me. If that branch breaks and you fall—"

"It is a strong branch. That's why I picked this place to sit."

"You will not be sitting anywhere in a few minutes," he muttered. "You will find it impossible to sit."

"Will I?" Cait sighed. "I much prefer sitting here to coming down there and getting my bottom spanked. If you want me to come down, you might have to bargain with me." She could almost hear him grinding his teeth.

"I might come down if you promise to hold me," she offered softly. His chest rose and fell. He looked at her with a look she didn't understand. "Why don't you hold me anymore, Duncan?"

"I do hold you."

"Not like you did before. You hold me like something that's fragile. Like something that's already broken beyond repair."

"That's not true," he said, but then fell quiet. His arms uncrossed and he put them on his hips in frustration.

"Come down!"

"No! Come and get me!"

With a curse he hiked himself into the tree. Cait watched half alarmed and half delighted as he scaled the branches more quickly than she ever could. He hauled himself to a stout bough just below her, and looked hard into her eyes.

"I miss you, Duncan," she whispered.

He took her in his arms and kissed her hard. She moaned. She didn't mean to, but to feel him really *touch* her again was almost too much to bear. Her soft pleading sounds seemed to inflame him, and his hands roved over her restlessly.

"Cait..." he sighed.

"Do you still love me, Duncan? I want to be your true wife, like I was before. If you still want me."

His gaze seared her. She thought he might take her right there in the cold branches of the tree. She would have welcomed him without complaint. But he began to climb down impatiently.

"Come with me. Now. To the room."

He jumped to the ground and practically yanked her out of the tree, leading her back to the keep at an unforgiving pace. When she became winded, he lifted her in his arms and carried her. She clung to his neck, breathing in his manly scent.

Up in his room, he let her down and she felt suddenly shy under his gaze. But she was determined to please him, to make him want her again the way he used to.

"Undress," he said. "Show yourself to me."

Cait complied, but she was conscious of the changes in her body, the pronounced bump at her waistline where she could feel the baby move sometimes, a flutter in her middle. Duncan came to her, running his hands over her new shape.

"The baby grows."

"Yes."

"It is a beautiful look for you. I hope...I hope..."

He looked troubled. She reached for him.

"I'm not afraid of bearing this babe. I'm more afraid of that spanking you threatened."

He smiled and pointed to the bed, tearing off his clothes.

"You should be afraid. You will get a spanking, but...my God. First things first. Lie down, wife."

She laid back and he came over her, kissing her passionately. He grasped her hands in his and pulled them over her head so she felt completely and totally controlled. Not controlled...*safe*. He wouldn't let go. She could feel his hard cock pressing against her, but she wanted it, she craved it. She thought for a moment of Lord Douglas pressing against her, forcing his way into her. This was not at all the same, although Duncan looked down at her worriedly.

"Okay?"

"Yes," she breathed. *Yes, please, please. Take me.*

"If I hurt you," he said, "let me know."

* * * * *

He was simply insane with desire. He wanted to plunge inside her violently, reclaiming her, making her his own. She sighed and moaned so sweetly under him. How had he resisted her charms for so long?

She wanted him. *She wanted him.* She clearly wanted him every bit as much as she had before. Why had he waited? Why had he denied himself? He wouldn't deny either of them a second more.

Chapter Sixteen

He slid inside her slowly, inch by inch, reveling in the feeling of possessing her again.

"Okay?"

In answer, she shifted closer, arching against him.

"Please, please..."

He withdrew and surged forward more deeply, drawing from her a shuddering moan. His free hand roved over her, cupping her breasts, bringing the dark pink nipples to his lips to suck and tease. She was so intense, so alive under him. He reached down to cup her bottom, to hold her fast for his demanding thrusts.

"Okay?" he rasped.

Her stifled groan signaled that she was as she writhed under him. She came a moment later, breathless and uncontrolled.

He released her and turned her on her stomach, pulling her onto her knees before plunging back inside. He held her hips in his hands, looking down at her shapely figure. In the light of day, he could see the fading scars there, thin stripes on her buttocks and back. But they made her no less beautiful to him, only more so. Her bravery, her desire, her refusal to give up when all seemed hopeless...her ability to forgive. He loved her. He needed her.

He had been foolish to deny himself that which he needed most on earth. Her smile, her laughter, her affectionate clinginess, he couldn't take these things for granted anymore. He couldn't hide away from her, hoping she wouldn't affect him. She affected him. It was a lost cause.

But it was okay, he thought as he drove into her, touching her deepest center, claiming her very soul. It was all okay, he thought as he shook with the pleasure of emptying himself inside her. With Cait, everything would always be okay.

He rubbed the small of her back as he lingered inside her, admiring the sight of her on her hands and knees. She began to shift, but a low sound from his throat stilled her, and she resumed her stance, back arched, head down. Only after a long moment did he withdraw his cock and back away. Even then, she lay still as he'd arranged her. He studied her pliant form thoughtfully, running his hand up her thigh to her bottom.

"How white and unmarked you are, Cait."

She made a faint sound into the bedcovers. He caressed the other shapely globe.

"There is still the matter of your punishment to see to."

She sighed softly. "I know."

He leaned close to her, breathing in the scent of her hair as he whispered in her ear. "You remember, of course, it is not to hurt you. It is not only done to cause pain. Not like him..."

"Yes, I know. I know you do it to help me be good."

"And because I love you."

"And because you love me. And care about me, and want me to be safe."

"Good girl," Duncan said. "You haven't forgotten."

No, she had never forgotten, although he had. Everyone had forgotten what love was all about. Everyone but Cait.

"Such a good girl." He lifted her hands from the bed to place them firmly on the headboard. "Such commendable obedience is rewarded. If you keep your hands there and remain perfectly still for the first ten strokes, you may take the second ten over my lap."

"Yes sir," answered Cait in a most submissive tone.

With a smile he lifted his leather belt from the floor and doubled it over. He didn't make her wait. And yes, he was perhaps a bit soft on her, but it had been a while since she'd taken any punishment, and she was several months pregnant besides. Still, he managed to give them just enough sting. She fought against the urge to fidget and dodge the blows, her fists going white-knuckled where they wrapped over the edge of the bed. She grew more and more tense, determined to please him. At ten, she sighed in relief.

Duncan laid the belt down, schooling his face to seriousness, playing his role. He would remain the firm disciplinarian until the punishment was over, although he was as pleased as she was at the prospect of continued punishment over his lap. He loved to see her struggling to take blows in position, or tied up, but he loved more to feel her squirm and tense across his thighs.

He sat on the bed and pulled her unresisting form across his lap. If she noticed he was obscenely hard again, she was far too well trained to let it show.

He marveled at how different she felt already as he held her, that extra softness she carried. He cradled her, holding her secure with one arm across her back. He spanked her, being careful to concentrate the force on the roundest part of her bottom. He felt the delicious conflict of wanting to enjoy every minute of spanking her, and at the same time wanting to rush through in order to impale her on his cock when it was done.

In the end he did both. He didn't dawdle, but neither did he rush. He gave her ten good, stinging spanks. Her tiny moans and wriggles drove him on.

He thought wryly to himself at the end as he pulled her up and lowered her onto his cock, that these punishments did much more than keep her safe. They did more than keep her obedient, show that he loved her...

For both of them, they did much, much more than that.

Chapter Seventeen

Duncan was at the practice field when he saw Edana ride into the courtyard. Even from his vantage point on the far rise, there was no mistaking it was her. The upright stance, the aura of power—even alone in the wild forests of Scotland, she was absolutely safe.

But not his wife.

His wife was not safe. Her time was almost upon her, and Edana showing up only magnified that fact. Cait seemed healthy and spirited enough for someone in her condition. But Lenore too had been healthy and spirited up until the last hours before she died.

He took his time making his way over to her, feeling each step bringing him closer to the end of this ordeal, his wife's pregnancy and the inevitable birth.

"Don't you look surly this morning," Edana murmured. "Not happy to see your dear mother-in-law?"

"Of course I am happy to see you."

"Only fretting about the reason I'm here."

Chapter Seventeen

"All husbands fret."

"Not all," said the priestess. "But the best ones do. Come," she said, holding out her hand to him. "Show me to my daughter. Let me see how well she is."

As they walked down the corridor to Cait's room, Edana questioned him about her recent habits and activity.

"Has she been eating well? Resting? Getting fresh air?"

"Too much fresh air. She's been gardening, walking about town, climbing blasted trees. I finally ordered her to her room a couple days ago, to preserve my own sanity."

"It's better that she's active. It's afterward that she must be made to rest. You have a nursery prepared, and nursemaids?"

"Yes, although I doubt Henna will allow anyone else to lay hands on the babe. Even me."

Edana laughed. "You will have your chance to hold your child, I promise you. It is best if fathers stay involved."

"Like Cait's father?"

Edana's smile faded. "That situation was not average. You should not pass judgment on situations you know nothing about."

"I judge no one," Duncan sighed. "I just want this over with. And I want Caitlyn to survive."

"I promise you, Duncan, I do too. And I tell you again, she will give birth with ease. I am more worried about you making a nuisance of yourself and scaring your poor wife out of her wits with your dire fears."

They stopped outside Cait's door. Edana looked at him sternly.

"You will wipe that frown off your face and smile at her and act as if you are at ease."

"I will not. You may visit her alone. Henna is within. I will leave these matters to the ladies, and return to the fields where I am more useful."

Duncan stalked away. He knew he'd been rude, but he wouldn't stay and smile and pretend total confidence when he was miserable with dread. He would smile when it was over, if things turned out all right.

And if they didn't...well. He was not even able to think about that.

* * * * *

Edana smiled to herself as she knocked on the door. What a singular man, this Devil of Inverness. What a sentimental mess.

There was only one man in a hundred who could put aside his own ego and selfishness to love a woman as he ought, and of those, fair few who loved and protected their wives perhaps even more than they should.

Lucky daughter of hers. She pushed open the door to find Cait smiling at her from the bed, surprised and pleased.

"Dearest Caitlyn," Edana greeted her warmly. "It is almost time, is it not?"

Cait's eyes shone with excitement. "Is it? I'll have the baby soon?"

"Yes, you will. Does Henna not tell you as much?" She nodded to the old woman in the corner, her own face alight with excitement.

"Oh, I tell the lass every day her time is near and she must keep to bed, but she won't," said Henna with a blustery sigh.

Edana sat at her bedside. "Let me look at this grandchild of mine waiting to be born."

She drew back the covers and laid her hands on Cait's swollen belly, pressing here and there carefully. "Head down I see. That's the best way. Does the baby feel low in your belly? Lower these last few days?"

"It feels low all the time," said Cait. "And today, the baby presses on my back so that it aches."

Edana smiled in approval. "It does come shortly then. Within days. Perhaps tomorrow. Perhaps even tonight."

"Tonight?" Cait echoed. "So soon?"

"It comes when it comes. Do you want a boy or a girl?" Edana said lightly to distract her.

Chapter Seventeen

"I want a little girl, although I think Duncan wants a boy."

I think Duncan will take anything so long as you withstand the birth, thought Edana to herself. "Well, if you wish to get out of bed into the fresh air, the best thing to do now is walk."

"Walk?"

"Yes, dearest, and I'll happily walk with you. Henna, help me pull her up."

*   *   *   *   *

Cait felt that she was waddling more than walking, but she tried to keep up with Edana as they toured Gordon's garden plots. Cait showed her the various plants and flowers she enjoyed tending, but she felt silly because she was sure Edana knew more of gardening than she could ever dream. Still, her mother listened and nodded in approval, taking time to congratulate Gordon on his crops. She pointed out helpful plants and flowers for use in healing and other household tasks.

"How do you know so much?" asked Cait.

"Years of training and study." She looked down at her daughter. "You might have studied the priestessly arts too, but you were a terribly sensitive child. I felt it was not the life for you. You were so shy, so retiring. I knew early on that you did not have the guile or hardness of conscience to be high priestess after me. Do you regret it? Would you have liked to study?"

"I don't know." Cait shrugged. "I like being Duncan's wife."

"And you'll be a mother soon as well. You are fortunate, much more fortunate than most women. Your husband loves you very much."

"Don't all husbands love their wives?"

Edana laughed. "Oh, you are an innocent indeed. I should say not. Some husbands at least care for their wives. Some do not even do as much as that. No, my Cait. You are one of the few to know love with the one you're wed to."

"Did my father love you?"

Edana blinked, but quickly composed herself.

189

"Well, you know, we were never wed, your father and I."

"But did he love you? Did he care about you?"

"We...I...we were like strangers on the night you...that we...the night you were conceived. But we understood one another at once."

"Understood one another? What does that mean?"

"Do you understand your husband?" Edana asked, turning the question back on her.

"I...I suppose I do. Yes. I understand him. What he wants. What he needs."

"I understood your father in the same way, although we were never so fortunate to find love."

"I know I am lucky," said Cait after a long pause. "I don't know why he loves me so much."

"Don't you? It seems clear enough to me. You have given your heart to him without reservation. You have loved the Devil just as he is, flawed and rough. He is no fool. He appreciates what you give to him so freely. He had another wife who was not nearly so kind."

"She died," Cait said quietly.

The two women walked a bit longer in silence.

"Are you afraid?"

"Yes," said Cait. "But I can't say so. Duncan is worried enough."

"Duncan will survive this birth, and so will you. I promise I will not leave your side until your healthy babe lies sleeping in your arms."

Cait's back ached again, and she stopped, leaning over.

"It hurts here?" Edana rubbed the exact spasming spot.

"Yes," Cait said tightly. "It really hurts. But that feels...that feels better when you rub it that way."

Her mother's knowing touch somehow made the excruciating tightness bearable again.

"Do you promise? Do you promise you won't leave me?" she whimpered through the pain.

"It would be better, perhaps," said Edana, "if we made our

way back to the keep."

* * * * *

God, the screams. He couldn't bear them. He paced the corridor, his men wisely keeping out of his way. There was the scream, over and over, and then the bitten off effort to stifle it. He wanted to tell her to go ahead and scream.

What he really wanted was to go back to nine months ago and leave her be, but he couldn't. It was far too late now. Even if he could, then she would now likely be bearing his father's child, which would have been even more impossible to take.

"Perhaps if you go to her," suggested Connor.

"Shut up."

"Just poke your head in and check on her. I assure you this is all perfectly normal."

"Shut up!"

Connor had five healthy children to his name, and sat placidly in the corridor while Duncan paced.

"The louder she gets, the closer she is," Connor said. "I'm sure it would comfort her to see you."

With a furious noise, Duncan turned and went to the stairs. Another bitten off scream propelled him faster.

"Where are you going?" asked Connor.

"Away! Downstairs!"

He couldn't bear the screaming any longer. It turned his stomach. It seemed like yesterday that Lenore had screamed, *Devil, get away from me!* He didn't want to be in earshot when Cait began to scream the same recriminations. He should be with her, but there was no way he could set foot in that room. He wanted to comfort her, but he couldn't bear for her to scream at him. He couldn't bear to see her suffer for what he'd done to her.

He was nearly to the hall when Edana's voice halted him.

"Duncan! You are needed at once!"

"Why?" He spun in a panic. "What is it? Why?"

"Your wife is calling for you! Don't you hear?"

He turned his head to the stairs, listening.

Duncan! Duncan, come to me!

"I can't go. You must understand, Edana—I can't bear it—"

"I do not care to hear what you can't bear," she snapped impatiently. "What of Caitlyn? How is she to bear it when the husband she needs, the husband she calls for is too selfish to come to her side?"

"Edana—"

"Come now. The baby will be born within the hour. Come to your wife's side and help her cope. The pain is terrible. She's tired. She's frightened. She needs your strength now!"

With a stifled curse, Duncan headed back to the stairwell. From the look on Edana's face he thought she would drag him herself if he didn't, and find success.

"Duncan! Duncan!" Cait cried his name between screams. "Duncan, where are you? Come to me!"

Devil, get away from me!

No, this wasn't at all the same.

He ran suddenly, ran to her as fast as his legs would carry him. He burst into the room to find Henna supporting her as she plodded unsteadily across the room.

"Why isn't she in bed?"

"Duncan! Help me!" Cait cried.

"Why aren't you in bed?"

"Just help me! The baby's coming—" Again she groaned, bearing down at Henna's urgent cries. Edana knelt to check beneath the blanket Cait clutched around her shoulders.

"Hold her, Duncan!" Edana said. "Support her so she can push the baby out. In a moment, Cait, when you feel the urge, you need to push, and you shall have a babe."

"I can't. I'm tired!" she sobbed.

"You can!" Duncan ordered. "You will." He braced her with his arms and held her when the next scream came. At Edana's urging, Cait ground her teeth and bore down.

"Carefully, carefully," said Edana, guiding the baby out. "There now," she said. "Duncan, help her to the bed. Let her lie down and rest while I tend to your beautiful new baby girl."

"My new baby girl?" Duncan echoed in amazement. "Cait, we have a daughter."

Cait looked back at him, proud and exhausted.

They had all survived.

* * * * *

Duncan watched in fascination as the women tended the baby. She was so weak, so tiny, although they insisted she was hardy as a soldier. They laughed fondly as she screamed at the top of her lungs.

"Listen to that temper," Henna said. "I remember a certain earl who wailed the exact same way when he was born."

Duncan smiled and pulled his sleeping wife closer into the shelter of his arms. "She may have my temper, but she is Caitlyn's daughter through and through, is she not?"

Edana stroked the baby's black shock of hair.

"She has Cait's hair, but her eyes favor yours, I think. She is a fine baby, healthy as the day is long. Your wife did well," she said with a hint of mother's pride. "Even *you* managed to survive the birth somehow."

Duncan barely registered her teasing comment. He was preoccupied by Cait sleeping in his arms, warm and tired and well and beautiful. She had survived. She had borne his child easily. Well, not *easily*. It didn't seem that way to him, although Henna and Edana went on and on about how smoothly the birth had gone.

The next one will be even easier, Henna had promised. *The first is the hardest.*

The next one? It was far too soon to think about it, but Duncan was glad to hear it would never be so difficult again.

Henna swaddled the baby girl and she finally quieted. She brought her to the bed, lying her gently down between Duncan and Cait.

"What will ya call the wee lass?" asked Henna.

Duncan looked at the tiny miracle between them. "I don't know. I think I had better wait until Cait awakens. I don't know much of girlish names. And I'm sure she'll want a say."

The baby squirmed and turned her head insistently, then just as quickly fell back to sleep.

"She can't decide if she wants to sleep or eat first," said Edana.

Duncan laughed. "Just like Caitlyn, sleep wins."

The low rumble of Duncan's laughter awakened Cait, and she looked around in confusion.

"Where is the babe?"

"Right beside ya, lass," chuckled Henna. "She's as tired as you are."

Cait looked down at her with a mother's wonder. Duncan watched the emotion flit across her face—surprise, adoration, and deep joy.

"Oh Duncan," Cait breathed, looking up at him.

"She's perfect, isn't she?" he whispered.

"Oh yes. Worth the wait."

Cait was too busy admiring her new daughter to notice the blush rising in Duncan's cheeks at that reminder of his foolish fears and delays.

"She looks just like you, doesn't she?" He smiled. "All that black hair. And her eyes are blue."

"What are we going to call her, Duncan?"

"I rather thought I'd leave that up to you. You'll need a bonny name for such a bonny lass as she."

"I'll have to consider on it a while," she said, yawning.

"And how are you, Cait? Do you feel all right?"

"I feel...perfect," she answered drowsily.

"Perfectly exhausted," teased Duncan. "Go back to sleep. I'll watch our daughter. You should rest."

"Okay, I'll try. But I'm really almost too excited to sleep."

Duncan laughed as her eyes began to shut again before she even finished her words.

"Duncan, thank you," she managed to murmur through the

haze of sleepiness.

"Thank you? You're thanking me?"

"For coming to me when I called you. I needed you, Duncan, and you came. I need you with me, always. Forever."

He stroked her face tenderly.

"Not nearly as much as I need you."

Chapter Eighteen

The baby was fed and changed and swaddled tightly, lain to nap in her tiny cradle.

"Sweet thing," crooned Henna as she rocked her to and fro. Cait smiled. The old woman could hardly abide to be away from baby Bonny for a moment, even now that nearly two weeks had passed.

"She sleeps, Henna. Go now and have some time to yourself."

"Oh, I don't mind watching her for ya. You go ahead. I'll come for you when she needs to be fed again."

"But you have watched her all day."

"Run along now," Henna insisted. "Go and visit with your husband. He'll be wanting to spend time with his wife."

Cait blushed.

"No, not that kind of time," Henna chuckled. "You don't let that man touch you that way for at least another month."

"Another month?" asked Cait with dismay.

"At least," Henna insisted. "Two months would be best. Six months, if you can manage it," she muttered hopelessly under

Chapter Eighteen

her breath.

Cait drifted from the room to go in search of her husband. Six months. She would not survive it. One month, perhaps, but it would be difficult. Anyway, she simply couldn't wait to have another baby, although Edana and Henna both urged her to rest and give it some time.

In fact, Edana had insisted Cait nurse the baby herself to prevent another pregnancy too soon. Henna had nearly fainted at the idea.

"It will tax her! And she is nobly born. It is not meet. We will get a wet nurse from the town."

"Pish posh!" Edana had dismissed that idea and brought the baby to Cait each time she needed to be fed. Cait loved feeding the baby herself, holding Bonny close as she suckled. Duncan would watch her—jealously, she accused—although he only laughed.

"It is not jealousy, but wonder."

"Wonder?"

"Wonder that I can share your beautiful breasts with anyone other than me."

Cait laughed at his teasing. Duncan was in a constant good humor now, smiling and content after so many months of frowns. And Cait, Cait definitely wanted another baby, the sooner the better. Motherhood suited her even more than she'd thought.

Six months. That was far too long to wait, and she was certain Duncan would back her up on that.

Cait emerged from the castle into the sunshine, Mitchum trailing at her heels. She stopped first at the orchard to choose an apple for Duncan. He would understand the invitation, although she doubted he would act upon it. Henna had poured cautions and threats in his ear, insisting he let her recuperate. He would have anyway, even without Henna's warnings, he was so protective of her. Oh well, she supposed it was endearing.

She headed toward the fields where she knew she would find him training with the other men. As she climbed up over the rise, she saw him walking towards her. And he was not alone.

She froze and nearly ran in the other direction. *Bonny.* She had to keep her baby safe. She had to hide.

Duncan raised his hand and waved, urging her to come and meet him and the man walking beside him.

Her father. The king.

Duncan waved her forward again impatiently. Panic warred with ingrained obedience, but finally, she forced her feet to move. She approached as closely as she could manage in her terror and dropped a short curtsy.

"Your Highness."

"Dear Caitlyn, there needn't be such formalities between us. Come and give your father a hug."

Cait stood where she was, gaping at the man as if he'd grown a second head.

"Duncan, perhaps Cait and I might walk a while and talk in private?"

She was already shaking her head, but Duncan nodded.

"Of course. You needn't ask permission of me to talk to your daughter."

Cait ran to Duncan's side and pulled on him. "Please don't leave me. Please!" she whispered.

He leaned down to look at her. "Cait, what is this fear? I promise you, he means you no harm."

"He does. He wants to kill me. He wishes me dead."

"He does not. Go to your father. He has come to see you and his new granddaughter."

Her eyes widened in alarm. "No, he cannot see her! He cannot take her away!"

"Cait, do you think I'd let any such thing happen?" He tilted her face up to his. "Go to the king. Do not keep him waiting. You're his daughter. You must not show him disrespect."

"Don't leave me alone with him, Duncan!" she pleaded.

"I won't. I'll wait right here with Mitchum. Now do as you're told. Do not embarrass me with this childish behavior. You may not be well enough yet to lie down with me, but I think I could give you a spanking if it were warranted, my love."

Cait turned reluctantly and walked back towards the king. He looked out of place away from his royal court and surroundings. Or perhaps the strange thing was that he did not look out of place at all. He was dressed in plain clothing, and he was alone, not surrounded by courtiers and advisors. In fact he looked a lot like Duncan and his men when they went about their everyday tasks.

"Caitlyn." He smiled warmly as she sidled up to him. "Come, walk a while with me."

She stole a look back at Duncan.

"I promise you could not be safer. I would not dare harm you even if I wished to. I think your husband would take brutal vengeance if I did."

Cait frowned, remembering Douglas. She fell into step beside the man who was her father, but she was still on guard.

"I see I have made you terribly fearful of me. I am sorry for that little charade at my keep. You rather caught me by surprise."

"Surprise?"

"Yes. Surprise. Shock. Panic. You see, I had very carefully and intentionally hidden you far from me and my world. Your mother helped too, of course. But then she thought I was keeping an eye on you, and I thought she was. When Erma sickened, neither of us knew it until it was too late. I'm terribly sorry. I would have spared you that fear and grief..."

His voice trailed off.

"I am sorry you felt abandoned and alone. And to make that dangerous journey to seek safety with your king, only to find... only to be told...well, I'm sure I hurt you deeply. You must understand why I said those things."

"I don't," said Cait stiffly. "I don't understand."

The king sighed.

"The daughter of a king and a high priestess like Edana has a value in the world. It's complicated, and you are probably too guileless to understand, but when you were born, many took an interest. The reasons for that interest varied depending on whom you were speaking to, but I will tell you, in some cases, the interest was for sinister reasons like ambition and greed. For Edana and me, that interest made us uneasy. When you were born you were secreted away for safety. But those with the basest, most selfish interest in you continued searching. When I learned that Edana was being threatened, that blackguards were lurking amongst the priestesses at the isle, we put it about that you had died. We mourned over a stillborn infant, buried you with a great, convincing display of heartbroken grief. All the while a small group of my most trusted soldiers were riding through the night to deliver you to Erma in the woods."

"Who was Erma? Why did you take me to her?"

"Erma was a great priestess at one time. Learned and capable. But in her older age, she wished to hide away. It presented the perfect opportunity for everyone. You got to live in safety and be priestess-raised, and Erma got the peace and serenity she longed for. You lived so sufficiently in the woods with her that I only occasionally sent a man to check on you. It was always a terrible risk, you see, and I told Edana so. She was the one who was supposed to keep in touch with you and Erma, but she had her own problems keeping the secret that you were alive. It seems we tried so hard to protect you that we ended up harming you unintentionally. I'm so sorry for that."

Cait's mind reeled. It was a lot of information to take in at once. The king paused, looking at her kindly.

"So you see, when they led you into my Counsel Room that terrible day, I suspected at once who you were, as did they. As you know, you are the very image of your mother. I could see it in their faces, the realization. I knew the gossip would spread quickly, so I pretended you were only a byblow of no consequence, the child of some worthless slut that I detested. I got you away as quickly as possible, to the safest, most far-flung keep I could think of. Again, it seemed that things worked out perfectly. I knew Duncan to be recently widowed, and I knew him to be a most upstanding and protective sort."

Cait stopped still, thinking over everything he'd said. "So it wasn't that you didn't want me? That you wished I had died?"

Chapter Eighteen

"Oh, my, no. You have no idea the guilt I've lived with, seeing that pain and suffering in your eyes when I uttered those words to you. But if I hadn't convinced my courtiers you were worthless to me, someone might have caused you mischief of a terrible kind. I had to get you to Duncan immediately. I couldn't even send you with adequate protection because that would have been seen as a sign of your worth. All of it, Caitlyn, it was all for your safety. But even here," he said sadly, "I'm told you were not entirely safe."

"No. Although that was no fault of yours or Duncan's. And I am better now."

"I'm glad to hear it. You look quite well and happy. It makes my heart unbelievably glad. You are pleased with your husband, and your life here at Inverness?"

"Oh yes, I love it here. And I love Duncan. He has been a wonderful husband to me."

"And now you are made a mother, mother of his child. Congratulations. I would love to see the baby."

Cait swallowed, overcome with emotion. "Of...of course you can. She is a girl, her name is Bonny."

"I hear she is the very image of you, just as you are the image of your mother."

Cait looked up at him, studying his face. "She is here, you know. Edana."

And she saw it, that same look she saw on her mother's face.

* * * * *

Cait walked back to the keep with the men in silence. As Duncan and her father discussed political and social concerns and other complicated things that men talked about, her mind drifted again and again to the same thought.

She had been wanted after all.

She had a father, just as she had a mother. They had both loved her all that time, all the time she had felt abandoned and alone. It was too strange to be walking here beside him, part of a family come together to celebrate the birth of a child.

At the door to the keep, Edana waited, stately and reserved. But her eyes, her eyes gave it all away. She came and embraced the king, and they clung to each other just a little longer than might be considered polite. Cait felt her throat close up with tears.

I understood your father, although we were never so fortunate to find love.

Cait thought it was terrible how circumstances could prevent people from being together with those they loved and cared about the most. She felt herself unwanted and unloved for so many years, but now she had a love that most could only dream of. A love the king and Edana could never openly share.

Duncan met her eyes, noting her pooling tears, understanding too. He cleared his throat, inviting them into the castle. The king seemed embarrassed by the reverence and obeisance of Duncan's household and servants, but Duncan insisted on a large, celebratory meal for the king and his men.

While preparations were made, the reunited family went abovestairs to introduce the bonny new baby to her royal grandfather. When Henna learned that the king was in her presence, she nearly fell to her knees.

"You musn't think of me as the king," he said to the old woman. "Just a doting grandfather come to see his new bairn." He peered down at the baby Cait placed in his arms.

"Oh, what a treasure." Wonder shone in his eyes. "What a treasure you have here, daughter."

"I know it, father. I know."

* * * * *

Cait watched from the window as her mother and father walked in the gardens under the cover of dusk.

"Stop spying," teased Duncan. "Let them be. They have not had enough time alone all these years."

"I'm not bothering them. I'm only watching. I just...I still can't believe it."

Duncan drew her from the windowseat, embracing her. "Someone as loving as you could only have been born out of love."

"In that case," Cait whispered, "Bonny will be loving too. The very lovingest bairn on earth."

"I sincerely hope so." He kissed her tenderly. "I'm sure she will be."

As his kiss deepened, Cait reluctantly pushed him away.

"What? What is it?"

"Henna says...that you are to leave me alone."

His laugh rang out so loud that Cait shushed him. "Duncan, you'll wake the baby!"

"And then Henna can put her back to sleep, and leave us alone. She is meddlesome, that old woman. And how long does Henna demand I let you be?"

"Six months."

"Six months!" he roared. Again Cait shushed him with a frantic fingertip pressed to his lips.

"She said one month at least," Cait whispered, "but that six months would be best."

"And what do you say, wife?" he whispered back, all devilish temptation now, his tongue coming out to lick her finger.

"I wish it were no time at all."

"Well, I believe there are many, many things we could do to each other that wouldn't harm you. And I think Henna would have told you so too, if she wasn't such an ornery old crone."

"Duncan!" chided Cait.

"Or if she didn't think we would resort to them on our own before too long. She may be ornery, but she is not stupid."

"You say I am naughty," she said as his hand made its way to the now-pulsing spot between her legs, "but I think you are generally the naughty one between us two."

"Perhaps. But you are the one who will end up over my lap getting her saucy bottom spanked."

She shrieked as he upended her, swatting her.

"Duncan!"

"Yes, dearest?"

"Let go of me!"

"I think I won't."

He swatted her bottom again, then ran his hand up her thigh, flipping the skirt of her gown up so she was bared to his gaze.

"What if Henna comes in?" she whispered.

"I guess she'll get an eyeful of your naughty behind, nice and spanked and red."

He smacked her again and then reached around the front of her to tap on the sensitive bud between her legs. She moaned as desire flared and spread.

"Now who's naughty?" he whispered.

"Oh, Duncan, please, please...touch me again, harder!"

"Here?" He pretended confusion, landing a smart slap to her buttock.

"Please!" she begged. "Between my legs!"

Again he only tapped and fondled her lightly, making her squirm and arch against his hand.

"Oh Duncan!" His hand soothed her now reddened cheeks, quieting her. She lay still, desperate to behave, to do whatever he wanted, if only he would touch her again. In time, her patience was rewarded as he again reached to stroke and tease her. This time, he alternated between firm slaps and delicious caresses until she fell apart, kicking and moaning in his arms.

"Hush," he said. "Be quiet or Henna will come."

"Quiet?" asked Cait when her breath returned to her. "I think they probably heard those spanks down in the hall."

"I'm sure they're relieved to know that the earl's naughty wife is getting exactly what she deserves."

He drew her dress down and pulled her to her feet.

"And now a naughty husband would like to get what he deserves. On your knees, Cait."

Epilogue

The buzzing of bees and the unseasonably warm sunshine made Duncan drowsy as he leaned back in the grass. His eyes flitted between his toddling son Alec and the two dark curly heads leaning together over the sand.

"An 'o' is next, Bonny. It's simple, like this. Just a circle."

The little moppet pushed her mother's hand away impatiently.

"Mama, I can do it. I can do it myself!"

"Yes, I see. Now the two n's are next. They're exactly the same."

"That's the easy part, mama."

"Yes, but don't write them backwards."

Cait watched as Bonny toiled over the sand with her stick, then looked over at Duncan. He was smiling indulgently.

"You don't mind, do you?"

"No, not at all. If her mama reads and writes, then she must too. And soon enough, you'll be able to teach this one," he said, swinging Alec up into his arms. The little blond boy squealed with laughter.

"Perhaps Bonny can teach her brother. Couldn't you, Bonny?" Cait prompted.

The almost-four-year-old wrinkled her nose. "He can't do it," she scoffed. "He can't do anything."

Duncan laughed at her saucy expression. "Every bit as naughty as her mother, that one," he said under his breath to Cait. "Tell me she's not."

"Oh, she's much naughtier than I was at her age. I think she's more like her dad."

Duncan put Alec down and swung Cait up over his shoulders instead, landing one sharp slap on her behind.

"What do you say we send the children back with Adele for their nap and go for a swim, just you and me?"

Cait peeked back at him shyly. "I think that sounds...nice."

"Nice?" he murmured. "Not exactly what I had in mind. Naughty, more like."

"Naughty?" whispered Cait as Adele came to lead the children away with a knowing smile. "Look, you've embarrassed the nurse again."

"I can't help it. It's all your fault. And now I'll have to force you to take off every stitch of your clothing and come pleasure me in the middle of the lake."

"You can be so unreasonably demanding sometimes."

"With such a wayward wife, I have to be. Enough talk. Disrobe."

She did, stifling a smile at the intent way his eyes followed her. She may have teased him just a little dawdling with the ties.

"Now my turn. Undress me," he said when she stood before him naked. His eyes scanned the trees around them as she took his clothes off. His men knew better than to intrude on their privacy at this particular lake, but he was cautious anyway. As soon as he was naked too, he led her into the water.

For a while, he was content to drift in the water and watch her swim around. She was like a fish, his wife. A lovely, beguiling fish. He dove under the water to grab her heels and surprise her. He could hear her scream even beneath the surface, and swam up

Epilogue

with a splash.

"That's not funny, Duncan! You scared me to death!"

"Come here." He ignored her indignant scolding and drew her to him. Since she'd borne him two children she'd become a lot more outspoken and brave in her ways, but he used it to his advantage most of the time. She wrapped her legs around him as he drew her arms behind her back and held them tightly there.

"I've got you, Cait," he whispered.

"I know. I like it when you have me," she admitted, nibbling at his ear.

"But will you like what I do to you?"

"I always do. Well, most of the time," she qualified, thinking of a particularly strict punishment he'd given her last week, when he'd tied her to the bed and pleasured her for over an hour, never allowing her to come. He had lectured her instead, and put her to bed with unsatisfied raving lust. It had been a difficult night.

But today, he was not out to discipline her. No, he had a decidedly different look in his eye.

He swam her over to a rock jutting out of the water and nudged her towards it.

"You know what to do."

Cait bent over the rock, arranging her hips just at the rounded edge where they fit most comfortably. She looked over her shoulder at Duncan, who was already nudging against her with his jutting cock.

He spread her open as she arched back against him. He dipped into her pussy first, slick with arousal, then withdrew. It took only a little effort to press inside her narrower passage, and she moaned as he drove all the way inside. Although she had long since learned that this method of lovemaking did not result in babies, she still enjoyed being taken this way every bit as much as Duncan enjoyed the taking.

"Give me your hands," he growled as she scrabbled for purchase on the smooth surface of the rock. She quickly offered them back to him and he took them firmly, holding them at the small of her back. "Good girl." He felt her relax, give herself up to his intimate invasion.

"Ohhh," she sighed. "That feels so..."

"So what?"

"So...naughty."

He growled softly as she ground back against him. "You would know." He rode her, stroked her, teased and caressed her until she was drawn up tight and tense. "Now come for me, Cait. I want to feel you come."

And she did as he asked, obeyed as she always did. They came together with great moans and sighs that Cait hoped couldn't be heard back at the keep.

Afterward they plunged back under the water and let it wash over them until they grew tired and made their way back to dry in the sun.

On the way, Cait paused to write again in the sandy shore *Will you love me always?*

And Duncan wrote back *I'll love you forever,* just as he always did.

About the Author

Annabel Joseph is a multi-published BDSM romance author. She writes mainly contemporary romance, although she has been known to dabble in the medieval and Regency eras. She is known for writing emotionally intense BDSM storylines, and strives to create characters that seem real—even flawed—so readers are better able to relate to them.

You can find Annabel's site and sign up for updates at www.annabeljoseph.com, or like her Facebook page at www.facebook.com/annabeljosephnovels. You can also find Annabel on Twitter (@annabeljoseph).

Annabel Joseph loves to hear from her readers at annabeljosephnovels@gmail.com.

Please enjoy the opening chapter of *Lily Mine*,
a Regency-era BDSM romance
by Annabel Joseph

Chapter One:
Lilyvale

Southeast England, mid-1820s

Lily trudged along the road to Lilyvale sustained by the kind of hope only the truly desperate possess. She *had* to find work. Gardening was her passion, but at this point she would settle for any household position she could get. She looked down at her basket of potted plants— passable chrysanthemums and cheery marigolds. They would not last much longer in the heat of the late-summer day, and then her investment in the blooms would be wasted. So far, she had given away three pots, but hadn't managed to procure a position. The mistress of the last manor had pointed her to Lilyvale, reportedly the home of a reclusive earl. Lily hoped the fact that she shared the name of the manor boded well.

A warm breeze ruffled her hair and the sturdy if threadbare lilac-colored muslin gown she wore. Her once-shiny leather shoes were dull and dusty from the road. Over the past three days she had walked all the way from Tunbridge to the outskirts of rural Kent, and while her feet protested, she was only too happy to put as much distance as possible between her and

London. If only she had the fortitude to walk on to Dover, she might cross the channel to Calais and begin a whole new life.

But then, she didn't speak French, and the Kent countryside was really quite lovely, a world away from London's dirty districts. Before long she was in sight of the manor house. It was a great stone structure, large for a country estate, with picturesque spires and battlements. There was a manicured garden to one side, and beyond it a large-sized greenhouse. The front of the manor was flanked by a long walkway which was also meticulously landscaped. However, the beds showed signs of neglect. The side garden needed weeding badly, and the rose bushes visibly drooped. Her heart soared with hope as she realized the earl could very likely be short of grounds help.

Aside from the gardens, there were a great many windows on the grand edifice. How wonderful to be able to look out at the grounds from any place in the house through those windows, and how bright and warm it must feel inside. Her family's London home had been dark and dank, crowded with noisy neighbors and foul city smells. She and her four sisters shared one cramped bedroom, which had led to many a shouting match. Although she'd never been very fond of her sisters, thinking of them now brought a mist of tears to her eyes. Lily shoved the sadness down, along with thoughts of her father's anger and condemnation.

Her father had blamed her for the loss of the Halstead household's account, the position that had kept him in the horticulture business practically since his start. Her father had designed and tended the Halstead mansion gardens in London for nearly two decades, and from a young age, Lily had gone along and helped out as his apprentice. Lily was the oldest of the five daughters, each named by their mother after a favorite flower. It was the Kendall matriarch who had truly lived for flowers and wanted to make the world bloom. But she had died birthing her youngest daughter, and Lily, a girl of ten at the time, had stood in her stead helping raise and nurture Rose, Violet, Iris, and baby Pansy.

That was, until last week when Lily had been sent away by her father, disowned and shamed. Lily had been ruined by Halstead's son, Lord Horace. *Ruined.* A horrible status for any young lady. She had never imagined such a thing befalling her, but now it was what she was. Ruined. The fruits of accepting a walk through a secluded garden with a rogue of a gentleman, and not realizing the peril thereof.

Horace had ruined her right on the ground, behind a berry bush her own father had planted. She had stared up at the vivid clusters of red fruit with a kind of hapless resignation at her plight. It wasn't as if there were marriage or a disappointed husband in her future—at twenty-one she had nary a beau to speak of, and was resigned to life on the shelf.

Anyway, there had been no point in struggling. Horace was a bear of a man and violently intent on what he was about. It had been painful but quickly over. She hadn't fought him as he rutted on her, his acrid breath blowing in her face. Afterward he had threatened her with her father's job if she told anyone. In the end, Lord Halstead let John Kendall go anyway, citing his daughter's loose morals as the cause of his dismissal.

Somehow, Lily had assumed her father would see through the lies of Lord Horace, but he had flown into a fury and tossed her out of the house. He denied her contact with her sisters, lest she corrupt them also. When she pleaded with him and asked how she was to survive without her family, he had thrown her a few coins and directed her to the south end of London where the prostitutes worked.

But she would not go there. She would not make her living "on her back" as her father suggested, not now that she had discovered what such a life entailed. She used what little money she had to gain passage to Tunbridge, and at Tunbridge did odd jobs while she looked for a position at neighboring households. She was offered kitchen and housemaid work at more than one place, but she wasn't quite ready to settle for that yet. She knew she could make a living with plants and flowers if she worked hard and didn't give up. She was smart and tough, and she was persistent. The time for tears was past. She had cried the entire way from London to Tunbridge, and cried a bit from Tunbridge to Smeeth as well, but she would allow herself no more crying.

And Lilyvale... She hoped it might turn her fates. Apparently the master of the manor was recently married and setting up house. Perhaps that explained the disarray of the gardens. With her experience and knowledge, she could have the grounds in elegant shape in no time. Lily squared her shoulders and walked to the side entrance, raised her hand and rapped on the door.

She waited several moments before rapping again more loudly. A few moments after that, despair began to set in. Was no one at home after all the effort she'd made to walk here? She was just about to give up when the door swung open and a tall thin manservant with a stern face popped his head out.

"Can I help you, miss—"

His voice cut off and his eyes widened as he stared at her. Lily looked down at the bodice of her dress for fear a great spider or beetle was crawling upon her, but she saw nothing to explain the servant's shocked face.

"Please, sir, if the head housekeeper is available, I have come to enquire after grounds work. I can do gardening and keep the greenhouse filled with flowers of every variety and color all year." She held up the basket over her arm.

Now the man's eyes narrowed. Why did he look at her that way? Before she could wonder very long, he made a move to withdraw back into the house.

"Wait here, miss. I'll return shortly."

"Oh, thank you, sir." The door was slammed in her face. What a terribly bizarre man. Lily was kept waiting a long while and had nearly given up a second time when the door swung open again. The man stood back and gestured her into the kitchen.

"Lord Ashbourne will meet with you in the front parlor."

"Oh!" Lily spun in confusion. "I did not mean to disturb your master. Can I not just speak to the housekeeper?"

"No, you may not," said the manservant in a rather affronted tone. "If you will follow me, please."

For goodness' sake, Lily was not at all used to rubbing shoulders with peers of the realm. The only lord she'd had acquaintance of thus far had very much wrecked her life. She was dressed in a messy, road-worn frock, and oh, her shoes were so dirty. She pulled and patted at her wind-tangled locks, trying to achieve some semblance of civility.

The servant led her down a long, wide hallway hung with imposing paintings of gentlemen and ladies. Members of the Ashbourne family, she supposed. They all peered down at her from their gilt-framed canvases as if to say, "Oh, what is *she* doing here?" Near the end of the hall, they passed a spot where a frame seemed to be missing, blank wall in its place. Lily thought on it only a moment before they passed into the grand foyer and her breath caught in her throat.

The foyer rose up above her in a high, open expanse of white with intricate pale blue and gold molding, and a spectacular wide staircase that curved around and up to the second floor of the home. A chandelier hung from a thick gold chain affixed at the height of the entryway's ceiling. It was like a constellation right there in the house, each crystal sparkling in the late afternoon sun slanting through the windows. She stared up open-mouthed at the hundreds of glittering orbs that comprised the fixture, until the servant cleared his throat.

"Right this way, miss."

Lily gathered her wits and followed him down another short hallway to a room on the left. The double doors were open. The servant stood back and Lily stepped into a large parlor in the same colors of pristine white and pale gold and blue. Several sofas and chairs were arranged tastefully around a low, marble-topped table. Lily noticed with hope that the wide table had no flowers on it—yet. In fact, there were no flowers at all in the staid room. It was an unusually uncluttered space. Some smaller tables contained light refreshments and a half-played game of chess. Windows along the front wall let in sunlight, which fell across the blue velvet upholstered chairs, making the surface of the fabric shimmer. In front of one of the windows stood a man who had to be the Earl of Ashbourne.

In the moment before he turned, she noted his height, the broad width of his shoulders, the proud carriage of his stance and his fine, well-tailored clothes. He wore dark trousers, topped with a midnight blue coat. His chestnut hair was cropped to a somewhat middling length, in the preferred style of the gentlemen in town.

At his man's soft cough, he turned to regard her. She waited for the impatient dismissal he was sure to voice when he realized his servant had arranged an audience with a disheveled commoner, but no curt words came, only a silent stare. His mouth was stern in appearance, and his jaw strong and angular, framed by an impeccably tied cravat. His face was striking, his nose prominent and not aristocratic at all. He had the look and mien of one who was powerful and masculine, and not that of the many dandy lords she'd seen about London. And the color of his eyes... Lily saw now why the entire house was outfitted in the pale blue of the sky, the blue of cornflowers in the sun. His eyes were a most remarkable shade of the same blue.

He was perhaps thirty years of age, although his grave expression made him appear older. As he approached, she realized that she must be staring. For that matter, he stared at her too, one hand rising to his mouth. She watched his finger trace over his lower lip and back as if he were deep in thought, or considering some puzzle. She dropped her gaze, befuddled by her reaction to his...beauty. There was no other word for it. Lily had been raised to appreciate beauty. The beauty of a flower, the beauty of a tree in bloom or a wonderfully designed garden. The beauty of nature.

This man was a gift of nature. He was just that beautiful to look upon.

"Your name, miss?"

Lily jumped as the manservant whispered the question in her ear. "Oh. It's Lily."

"Lily, a gardener," the man boomed out as if they were not, the three of them, alone in a silent country parlor.

Lord Ashbourne looked at his servant with something like exasperation, then inclined his head as Lily curtsied. She had learned gentle manners and speech from her mother, but still she wasn't sure what to say or do in this singular situation. She was relieved when Lord Ashbourne gestured to the nearest divan.

"Please, sit down."

Lily took a deep breath and crossed to sit on the velvet cushions, being careful to set her basket down so no dirt or soil fell in the immaculate room. She looked up again at the lord of the manor. She must wait for him to speak, mustn't she? But he had fallen silent again, staring at her no less intently. The servant left, shutting the double doors with a click that echoed in the stillness. She swallowed hard, quite ill at ease.

"Well, sir… Erm… My lord, I am so very sorry to disturb you."

"It is no disturbance. I was not busy. Why have you come to Lilyvale this afternoon?"

His tone was strained, as if he were frustrated but trying to keep it in check. He did not sit down but stood, facing her, bracing his hands on the back of the opposite divan. She noted that his knuckles were nearly white in their grip. She would be quick. She did not want to keep him if he was in a temper.

"My lord, I have come to seek employment with your grounds staff, to beautify your lovely manor."

"Lilyvale has no grounds staff at present, I'm afraid."

She bit her lip. He was definitely not in a good mood. Then again, she had been around so few of his type. Perhaps this clipped, tense formality was just the way all wealthy gentlemen acted. "I wouldn't wish to take up your time," Lily said. "I might just as well speak to the lady of the house, or your housekeeper if it pleases you."

"The lady of the house is away and the housekeeper is off for the evening, so I suppose you might just as well speak to me."

A part-time housekeeper? She blushed, realizing he must have fallen on hard times like so many of the gentry these days. Gambling, bad debts, unfortunate investments. She was not likely to find employment here now, if he didn't even have the funds to adequately staff his household. His uncluttered and austere parlor was thus explained. She looked up at him, hoping the blush didn't show too much in her face. She forged ahead only because she had no idea how to leave at this point with any grace.

"I am an experienced horticulturist, sir, come recently from London. My father and I provided service for a well-regarded family of Bond Street, so if you've a need for a gardener to aid you, I am quite capable of serving a grand estate such as this."

He gave her a long, assessing look. "It is unusual, is it not, for a woman to work in groundskeeping?"

"Not so much anymore, my lord, if you'll pardon my saying. Mrs. Wells Loudon has recently popularized gardening for women, and I have worked as my father's assistant for years. I am particularly interested in the cultivation of exotic flowers."

"Flowers must certainly benefit from the delicacy of a woman's touch." He strolled around the divan and took a seat opposite her, seeming to relax somewhat from his earlier state. He cocked his head to one side. "You were named for a flower, I gather. The delicate lily of the valley, or the showier calla lily? Perhaps the tiger lily?" His lips turned up in the very shadow of a smile.

The way he said *tiger lily* made her blush. Surely this was most irregular, for the lord of the manor to sit and converse with a tradeswoman this way. Perhaps she was in some danger here. Her misuse at the hands of Lord Horace was still fresh in her mind. Perhaps all these privileged lords just took what they wanted with no thought to consent. She cast a look at Lord Ashbourne from beneath her lashes. He did not have the predatory look Lord Horace had when his gaze had followed her around. In fact, Lord Ashbourne still looked quite stern and almost…sad. She thought again of his money difficulties. What a mess she had made, ruining his day by offering services he couldn't afford.

"My lord, please forgive me," she said, rising. "I made a mistake in coming here. I have disturbed the solitude of your afternoon. I won't keep you any longer."

"The solitude of this and every afternoon grows tiresome," he cut in. "Please do not go. Not yet."

She sank back onto the velvet divan and took some deep breaths, calming herself. He was not threatening her, although his attitude did seem rather commanding. His wife was away and he was apparently bored without her, but that did not mean he wished Lily harm. She clasped her hands in her lap and tried to exude calm amiability in her smile.

"Tell me about these flowers you've brought." He gestured to the basket at her feet. "Are these some of your greenhouse flowers?"

"Oh, no sir. I haven't my own greenhouse yet."

"Yet?" He seemed mildly amused by that. She lifted her chin.

"I know it is not common for women to be in trade, but I hope to have my own greenhouse and flower shop one day. It is an ambition of mine."

"I have great respect for ambitious women, Miss Lily. In fact, I would like to purchase some flowers from you. What is the cost of the flowers you have there?"

"Oh! You may have them if you wish. I brought them as a sample of my work."

"Nonetheless, I would prefer to pay you."

Lily looked down, and the simple potted blooms suddenly seemed rather pathetic compared to the rich, understated luxury of Lord Ashbourne's sitting room. She named a price that was probably too low but she couldn't bear to charge more, especially with her suspicion that her host was not well in the black. His expression darkened at her price and she nearly spit out a lower sum, but he interrupted her by calling for his man and sending him for the coin. She hoped she had not ruined the opportunity to gain employment with him, bartering over half-wilted flowers.

"I particularly love the brightness of marigolds," he commented quietly, just as she was thinking how shabby they were. His kindness cheered her.

"I love marigolds too. They come in so many shades and colors. In London we managed to propagate a stunning yellow-red variety."

"Are marigolds your favorite flower?"

"No, my lord. I am partial to bulbs, but they are not in season now. There are so many beautiful ones. Daffodils, tulips, lilies."

"Ah. I am partial to lilies myself."

"Yes, my lord." She flushed, feeling stupid. He was staring at her with the strangest preoccupied expression. Then he abruptly sat up.

"Will you come back, say, tomorrow? I will be assembling a gardening staff soon and I could certainly use an experienced horticulturist like yourself."

"Why—yes. Gladly, my lord. You would not be disappointed in my services, I promise it, even if I am not a man."

Hanover, the servant who had first admitted her, returned with a leather purse and handed it to Lord Ashbourne. He shook out a handful of coins and crossed to drop them into her palm. She could not have counted them in front of him like some money-scrabbling merchant, but it was obvious he'd paid too much.

"Sir, are you certain this accounting is correct?"

"I paid a bit more to thank you for your trouble. Lilyvale is well off the beaten path and I appreciate you taking the time to come here."

Lily thought she should protest but she pocketed the coins instead, thinking of a warm bed at the inn at Smeeth. *No.* She needed to save, she needed to put away just in case. Her employment was still uncertain as yet. She dropped a curtsy.

"I appreciate your generosity so much, sir. I'll come by again tomorrow, I promise. It's not much trouble. The road here is lovely to walk along."

"Do you think so?"

He was standing at least an arm's length from her, but something in his gaze suddenly felt inappropriate. He was such a large man, and stood so straight and unyielding. His eyes were so intent. His arms at his sides looked tense, as if poised for action. She remembered the stance from another moment in time. She remembered how Lord Horace had looked at her just moments before he dragged her behind the bushes. Her cheeks flooded warm and her blood rushed faster. *Foolish girl, tricked again!* She had accepted his extra coin and now he would expect something in return. Her throat drew tight as he leaned closer.

"If you like, why not have a cool drink with me before you go? It's a warm day and I've offered you no refreshment."

"No!" Oh dear, she had practically shouted at him. She softened her voice and sidled for the door. "Thank you, my lord, but please do not trouble yourself."

What a thing to do, to invite a common girl like her to take tea alone with him in his parlor. It was clear to her now that he was after the same prize Horace had stolen from her by force. She infused her voice with all the authority she could muster.

"I really must be going, my lord. Though your kindness has been heartwarming, I must take my leave. At once."

Lord Ashbourne nodded, still studying her in a most unsettling manner. "Of course. I suppose you must return to Smeeth before evening comes on too strong."

"Yes, sir. Exactly."

"I would be happy to lend you the use of my carriage."

"Oh no, please." It got worse and worse. She needed to get away, and quickly. She prayed that he wouldn't press the issue. Fortunately, he conceded and bowed his head.

"Very well."

Oh, he was doing that strange frown again. Now she had offended him! She was making an absolute muck of everything.

Why did he fluster her so much? It was the way he looked at her with those direct, unfathomable expressions.

"It…it was a kind offer," she said, trying to continue on assertively. "But I do enjoy the fresh air."

"Of course. It was only a suggestion. Well then, Miss Lily. Good evening to you." He stood back and gestured to Hanover, who handed over her now-empty basket. She stole one last look at Lord Ashbourne and he nodded to her somberly as she took her leave with another curtsy.

He was a beautiful man, she couldn't deny it. But even beauty like that, even the promise of more coin could not compel her to lie under him and endure what she'd endured at Horace's hands. Lord Ashbourne was even bigger than Horace, much more fit and virile. If he laid his hands on her she would not be able to get away.

No, it was best to leave and do any further business with the housekeeper or Lady Ashbourne. Hopefully they would be in attendance tomorrow, for she did not want to give up possible employment simply because of his overly familiar ways. As she started down the path away from Lilyvale, she remembered the coins in her pocket and reached in to ascertain if he had really overpaid her as she suspected.

Oh, good heavens—he had paid her three times what she asked for! It had been an anxious visit, but worth her time. She ignored the rumble in her stomach and trudged down the road until she found the shady clump of trees where she had stowed her cloak and satchel. She sat and took off her shoes and stockings to rub her aching feet and think.

Lily Mine is available in paperback at Amazon.com and in ebook format wherever romance ebooks are sold.

Made in the USA
Lexington, KY
26 December 2012